TURNED ON

Stacy was too occupied with thoughts of Nick to care whether her classmates approved of him or not. Nothing could come between them. They had different backgrounds, different friends, different interests, but their interest in each other was something they shared deeply. The electricity had been powerful the moment they met, and it grew stronger every day.

Nick would phone, and the huskiness of his voice would make Stacy feel so weak she'd have to sit down. They'd brush against each other, and her skin would tingle. The chemistry between them was deliciously, dangerously explosive. She was fascinated by everything about him.

Stacy had always been a winner. Now she'd won the wrong boy.

THE
GIRL MOST
LIKELY

Suzanne Rand

BANTAM BOOKS
TORONTO · NEW YORK · LONDON · SYDNEY · AUCKLAND

RL 6, IL age 12 and up

THE GIRL MOST LIKELY
A Bantam Book / November 1985

ISBN 0-553-25323-9

Published simultaneously in the United States and Canada

Bantam Books are published by Bantam Books, Inc. Its trademark, consisting of the words "Bantam Books" and the portrayal of a rooster, is Registered in U.S. Patent and Trademark Office and in other countries. Marca Registrada. Bantam Books, Inc., 666 Fifth Avenue, New York, New York 10103.

PRINTED IN THE UNITED STATES OF AMERICA

O   0 9 8 7 6 5 4 3 2 1

This college-bound blond beauty can be seen leading the cheers at all the Midvale games . . . one of our best-dressed seniors, Stacy turns up her nose at anything "grubby" but can't get enough of the pepperoni pizza at Nicola's . . . swimming and tennis rate high with the girl who rates highest with everyone . . . there's no doubt this is the girl most likely to get whatever she wants in life.

Entry under Stacy Harcourt's
senior picture in *Midvale Memories*,
the high-school yearbook.

ONE

"Welcome to the first cheerleading practice of the year. It's good to see all of you again." Ms. Donna Bowen, Midvale High School gym teacher and coach of the Midvale cheering squad, stood in front of the six girls sitting in two rows of the gym's bleachers—three seniors in front, three juniors behind them. In her gray leotard and nylon gym shorts, Ms. Bowen didn't look much older than the girls seated before her. Only the streaks of gray in her wavy brown hair revealed that she was not a student.

Hands on her hips, she challenged them: "Are you raring to go?"

"Yes!" six voices shouted in unison. Stacy Harcourt grinned at Tess Belding, who was sitting next to her, knowing Tess felt the same excitement that energized her. The first day of cheerleading practice was even more exciting than the first day of school itself. And this year promised to be the most exciting ever. This year they were seniors.

"Way to go!" Ms. Bowen smiled in satisfaction at the group's enthusiasm. "We'll begin practice by seeing how well the six of you kept in shape over the summer. But first let's hear from our new squad captain. Stacy, come over here and fire these girls up!"

Stacy sprang to Ms. Bowen's side. Her voice bubbled with enthusiasm. "It's great to be back in school again," she began, "and I know you all want the same thing I want—to make the Midvale football squad the best in the state this season!"

She broke off, smiling, as they applauded her words. The other five girls, the winners of one of the most important competitions at Midvale, were cheering her, Stacy Harcourt. She just adored being captain.

"Most of us have been cheerleaders in the past, on this squad or on the J.V. squad. But not all of us." Her eyes scanned the two rows, resting briefly on Kathy Phillips, a junior and the only girl on the squad with no cheering experience. Kathy had let her hair grow longer over the summer; it was easy to see the blond eleventh-grader was doing everything she could to copy Stacy's own hairstyle. Stacy gave her a special warm smile.

"Now, you juniors had just made the squad when the election for captain was held last spring, so some of you don't know me as well as others. You'll get to know me a lot better this semester. I hope you'll want me to keep heading the squad for basketball season. I may not do the best jumps"—she looked over at Gina Damone, who was undeniably the best female gymnast in the whole school—"but I hope you'll agree the school picked someone with leadership ability."

She had more to say but paused again as the girls applauded wildly. *It's true*, Stacy thought confidently. *I am the best leader, and I can make this squad the best ever*.

At least she was doing a good job so far. Admitting the obvious—that she wasn't best at jumps—was a nice way of giving Gina a pat on the back and also of showing that she didn't have a swelled head. Of course, everyone knew Stacy had won the captain's election by a landslide, and everyone knew why, too. Stacy was one of the most popular girls in the school, maybe the most popular now that she was captain.

But knowing all along that she'd be voted captain of the squad in her senior year—she'd been J.V. captain during her freshman and sophomore years—didn't mean she had the right to act smug. She'd seen other girls lose their popularity because of conceit, girls like Valerie Masters, the head majorette. Valerie was almost as pretty as Stacy, with the same willowy figure, and at one time last year, some girls were dying to be part of Val's exclusive circle. But Valerie had let popularity go to her head and had become obviously fickle and unfaithful to her friends. As a result, although she was still powerful and popular on the surface, most girls tried to stay out of her way and gossiped about her in her absence.

I won't be like that, Stacy vowed as she pulled a slip of notebook paper from her pocket so that she could read the schedule of cheers. *I'll never change.*

"We've got plenty of time to work through all the cheers and get these routines letter-perfect before the first game," she assured the squad members, all of whom were hanging on her every word. "Today, Ms. Bowen and I agree we should just try to warm up and get back in the swing of things. That means we'll be doing some stretches first, then our high kicks and splits. Whatever you do, don't push yourselves too hard today. We don't want anyone sidelined with a torn muscle. We'll finish up with basic jumps: back jumps, high jumps, split jumps. Then some song practice. The only cheer we'll do all the way through today is 'We're the Midvale Mustangs.'

"One other thing before we start. I think all of you know how important we are to the school as cheerleaders. Let's not forget that being on the cheering squad means more than going to practice and cheering at the games. We've been picked out as the ones everyone else looks up to, and it's part of our responsibility to set a good example, be class leaders, stir up school spirit and keep it high. Don't ever forget that we're cheerleaders twenty-four hours a day, whether we're in uniform or not. And we're representing Midvale High School all the time, everywhere we go. Now, let's practice so we'll be the best in all of Illinois when the first game rolls around!"

Although everyone was a little rusty, it was a good practice. Stacy was glad to see that the other girls waited for her comments on their skills and looked to her for approval. She was the natural squad leader.

After practice, as the squad changed back into their street clothes in the locker room, the other girls clustered around Stacy.

"What do you think of the new uniforms?" Pixie, one of the juniors, asked. "You'll look the best of all of us. Blue and gold are perfect for blond hair and blue eyes like yours."

"I like them better than those jumpers we had last year. And I deserve a uniform I look good in!" Stacy laughed. "That mustardy gold color from the old uniform made me look utterly, absolutely jaundiced."

"You couldn't look bad if you tried," Sherri Callahan said enviously. Stacy smiled modestly. "Really, Stacy, just look at yourself in the mirror. I'm all sweaty and my hair is a mess. You look as good as you did when we started out." She sighed with resignation.

Stacy laughed happily, swinging her honey-colored hair so that it spread across the shoulders of her blue cotton sweater. "Come on, don't try to butter me up. Ask Tess how ratty I look when I get out of bed in the morning!"

"Are you coming to Nicola's for Cokes?" Gina Damone asked eagerly, her enormous dark eyes anxiously awaiting Stacy's answer. The hint of an Italian accent left over from earliest childhood grew more pronounced when Gina was excited. "I'm riding with Tess."

"Of course I'm going to Nicola's. It's practically a cheerleading institution. We have a tradition to uphold. I can't stay long, though," Stacy added as she grabbed her shoulder bag and walked toward the mirror to reapply her lip gloss. "Rich has football practice, of course, but he's picking me up right after dinner, so I've got to do my chemistry homework first." She groaned.

"Guess what?" Tess Belding scurried up next to Stacy to smooth clear gloss over her bright red lipstick.

"I give up. What?" Stacy smiled. Although she was used to her lifelong best friend's perpetual animation by now, Tess's clumsy enthusiasm never failed to make her smile. Her smile broadened as Tess dropped her makeup bag in her excitement, and a vast array of lipsticks, blushers, and eye pencils scattered over the floor.

"Oh, darn it all! Why am I always all thumbs?" she moaned, bending over to retrieve her cosmetics.

"Because," Stacy told her, dipping down gracefully to pick up a mascara that had rolled against her foot, "you wouldn't be Tess otherwise. Why worry about it? You know everybody thinks it's cute when you get flustered."

"That's easy for you to say," Tess muttered. But she was smiling, and she didn't look as if anything could bother her today. "You never lose your cool. You Harcourts must inherit it."

"Anyway, guess what *what?*" Stacy put away her gloss and led Tess back to her opening line.

A look of confusion clouded Tess's soft features momentarily. Then she remembered. "Oh! Dave Prentice asked me out again. For this weekend. I said yes. That was okay, wasn't it? I mean, do you think I'm acting too available? Should I turn him down and play hard to get now that we've had a few dates?"

"Of course you shouldn't!" Stacy hugged her. "That's terrific, Tess! Do you know how many girls in this school would sacrifice their eyelashes for a date with Dave?"

"Yeah, I guess they would." Tess's voice grew dreamy. "He's gorgeous, isn't he? I still can't believe he's interested in dopey Tess Belding."

"I wish you wouldn't put yourself down all the—"

Tess cut her off. "I know, I know. And I appreciate all the self-confidence pep talks you give me. But I still can't believe it. Anyhow, I was thinking, maybe the four of us could double-date again soon. You know, you and Rich and Dave and I."

"Maybe," Stacy said vaguely. "We'll have to see. Come on, let's get going. Gina must be tired of waiting for you, and if we don't get to Nicola's soon, I won't have time to do anything but run in and run out. We'll talk about it a little later on, okay?"

Tess had looked a little hurt at being brushed off, Stacy realized as she crossed the parking lot to her car. Well, Stacy just couldn't talk to anyone about it right now. She would explain soon, maybe even tomorrow.

Right now, she just had to keep quiet, in case she changed her mind. But unless Rich managed to really sweep her off her feet tonight, she was kissing him good night and goodbye forever this time.

This was her senior year, the most important year of high school—maybe of life itself. Stacy was already cheering captain and would probably be winter carnival queen in January and prom queen in May. Nothing was going to keep this from being the happiest, most exciting time of her high-school career. And that meant that, as loyal and devoted as Rich Stinson was, he was history if she expected to make her dream come true.

"I don't get it, Stacy. You say you don't want to go out with me anymore, right? And now you say you don't have a reason for feeling that way. You're not making any sense!"

Rich Stinson sighed deeply. In the light from the dashboard, the misery and confusion he felt showed clearly on his handsome features. He looked so vulnerable it was all Stacy could do to keep from taking back everything she'd just said. *But if I do that,* she reminded herself bluntly, *I'll be stuck right back where I was three painful hours ago.*

"It doesn't make a lot of sense to me, either," she admitted, her voice low. "But I know I'm right. We're just not—well, not *right* for each other, Rich. What we've got is great. Only, it isn't enough."

"How can you say that?" he asked, sounding almost angry. "Great's great, isn't it? How can great not be enough?"

"Oh, darn you, anyhow! Do you think this is easy for me?" she asked, her angry tone rising to match his. Why couldn't Rich let this scene happen as gracefully as she had planned it? "What I mean is that I care about you an awful lot, Rich, but I need something more. And I know it's more than what we've got."

"If that's how you want it, I guess there's nothing I can do about it," he said coldly as he turned the ignition key and the engine whirred into life. "C'mon, I'll take you home."

As Rich backed the car out of the grassy space by Brinton's Lake where they'd been parked, Stacy saw the closed, defiant look on his face. Still, the slump of his normally broad shoulders left no doubt that this evening's turn of events hadn't been his choice.

Stacy knew she wasn't being fair. She hadn't given Rich any more explanation than that she was bored and dissatisfied. But what could she say that wouldn't make him feel even worse? How could she tell him that she was breaking up with him because she didn't hear bells when he kissed her, didn't go weak in the knees when their eyes met across a classroom, didn't feel bolts of electricity coursing from his body into hers whenever they held hands?

No, she thought as she sank deeper into the passenger side of the small car, *sometimes it's better not to tell the whole truth.* Any further explanation would just make Rich feel awful.

So Stacy kept quiet, and Rich's temper cooled as quickly as it had flared. By the time he came to a stop at the curb in front of the fieldstone path leading up to the Harcourts' three-story, white Colonial house, his lips had curved into something that was almost a smile.

"Well, Stace," he said with an attempt at lightness, slipping an arm casually around her shoulders, "it was fun while it lasted."

"Oh, Rich, I'm so glad you don't hate me!" Stacy was relieved that Rich wasn't going to beg or plead or make a last-chance scene on her front porch. "I'm really sorry it has to be like this. It's just—" She shrugged, unable to find the right words, the words that wouldn't wound him. "Who knows?" she said at last with a nervous giggle. "Maybe I'll end up deciding you were the right guy for me all along."

"Maybe I'll be waiting if that time comes," he whispered, breaking off to let his lips brush hers ever so gently, "and then again, maybe I won't."

"I understand, Rich," Stacy said automatically. "And I hope we'll always be friends."

Then she hurried from the car and up the path, not turning to look back over her shoulder and wave as usual as Rich accelerated back onto Hawthorne Lane with a scattering of gravel.

Stacy did sincerely hope that she and Rich would always be friends, not just because she liked him, but because Stacy Harcourt hadn't become one of the most popular seniors at Midvale simply by virtue of her pretty heart-shaped face and mane of naturally streaked blond hair. She knew it made plain good sense not to make enemies, certainly not enemies who were both popular and powerful at Midvale High School.

The cars she saw lined up in the wide double driveway meant her parents' bridge party was in full swing, so instead of letting herself in at the front, she continued around the side of the house, digging into her soft leather shoulder bag for her door keys.

Normally Stacy didn't mind her parents' friends; in fact, she liked most of them. But this night she didn't feel like stopping to make small talk with the couples who'd be seated around the card tables set up in the living room. She quietly made her way up the back staircase.

She turned off at the second floor and walked down the familiar dimness of the wide hallway, past her parents' bedroom, bath, and dressing rooms, and past the guest rooms, to the other side of the wide main staircase. Her room and her sister, Sarah's, were here, joined by a connecting bathroom. Across the hall was the housekeeper's room as well as the old nursery, which had been turned into a den for doing homework once she and Sarah had grown too old for the toys and puzzles that still filled its shelves and drawers.

Stacy had this wing practically to herself now. Sarah, a junior at Chatham College in upstate Michigan, came home only for an occasional weekend and longer school breaks. When she opened her bedroom door, Stacy was greeted by the soft glow of the luminous digits on the clock-radio that sat ringed by perfume bottles on top of the white dresser that matched her canopied twin beds. *Only ten o'clock,* she thought with a sigh as she absent-mindedly flicked the wall switch and bathed the room in lamplight. Even on a school night, ten P.M. was awfully early to be going to bed.

But there was nothing else she wanted to do. There wasn't much homework to do this early in the school year. She'd finished her chemistry problems and had already read the latest magazines on her bedside table from cover to cover. It was too late to pick up the white Princess telephone on the table and punch in Tess's number to relate the evening's events; Tess's dad got up at six in the morning, as her own father did, to commute into downtown Chicago, so the Beldings frowned on late-night phone calls. Stacy had tried to convince Tess to pay for her own private line like the one Alexander Harcourt had given his daughter for her sixteenth birthday, but Tess preferred spending her own generous allowance on clothes and makeup.

The morning would be soon enough to spread the word that she was a free woman, Stacy decided as she slipped out of her cotton jumpsuit and into a freshly ironed flannel sleep shirt. Besides, Stacy wasn't sure she could explain her actions to Tess any better than she had to Rich. Now that she'd actually done what she'd been thinking of doing for weeks, now that she'd actually broken up with Rich, she wasn't sure she felt like triumphantly announcing the news to her friends. If anything, she felt strangely nervous.

Well, you wanted to shake your life up a little bit, kiddo, she told herself, closing the windows partway to let in less of the cool night air. One of her favorite knickknacks sparkled at her from the top of the low cabinet that held her records, stereo, and portable color TV, and she picked it up as she passed.

The object Stacy studied was a block of clear

glass about four inches square. When Stacy had spotted it in August in the window of one of the gift shops at the mall, she'd known immediately that she had to have it, even though the price sticker on its side told her it would end up costing more than a week's worth of her spending money. But she couldn't resist. Never before had she seen anything that represented her own life so completely.

She held the cube up to the little milk-glass shade of her bedside lamp as she stretched out on top of the white ruffled spread.

Trapped inside was a beautiful butterfly with wings of iridescent turquoise and jade. It was exactly as Stacy often saw her own life— glamorous but going nowhere, frozen forever in static perfection. The day she had brought home the butterfly was the day she'd first begun thinking about not seeing Rich anymore, even though for the seven months they'd been dating, he'd never done a single thing to make her unhappy.

But not being unhappy, Stacy told herself, *isn't the same as being really happy, isn't the same as being truly alive.*

Stacy set the butterfly on the table and contemplated her future as she finished getting ready for bed. It had never occurred to her she might feel this way—scared and already wondering if she'd done the right thing—when she finally said goodbye to Rich.

What if the excitement she'd dreamed about

wasn't waiting for her? What if she didn't fall madly in love with somebody new, ever? Worse, what if she never had another date as long as she lived?

Stacy smiled in spite of the momentary flush of anxiety that had swept over her. Hadn't Dex Grantham given her a cool, appraising once-over just the other day in algebra class? And Rich or no Rich, Stacy was in control of her life. She was captain of the cheering squad for football season, and she was a shoo-in as captain for the basketball and baseball seasons. She'd be voted winter carnival queen; by tradition, a cheerleader always won. And she didn't have to worry about getting accepted when she applied at Chatham.

But *some* things were going to change. She could feel it. As she reached over to turn out the light, her eyes paused on the butterfly. Poor butterfly, it was destined to go nowhere. But not Stacy Harcourt.

For better or for worse, Stacy was busting loose.

TWO

"You did what?" Tess's voice squeaked the way it always did when she got excited, and her blue eyes widened.

Stacy grinned across the cafeteria table at her best friend. With her latest curly perm, a heavy dusting of bright pink blusher, and dark eyeliner applied with a too free hand, Tess looked just like the cartoon character Betty Boop. Of course, Stacy would never say such a thing out loud. Poor Tess fretted so much about her looks.

"You heard me," she said calmly. "Last night I told Rich I don't think we should see any more of each other."

"But how come? He wasn't fooling around behind your back, was he?"

"Don't be silly!" Stacy made an airy dismissing motion with her left hand. Her other hand held a fork, poised now to scoop up another mound of tuna salad. "It's like I told Rich—I can't really explain it. But I just—" She sighed and shrugged her shoulders. "Well, haven't you ever felt that what you've got isn't enough?"

"Sure," Tess said quickly. "I feel that way all the time. Only, I'm not Stacy Harcourt, the girl who's got everything, so it's not unusual." Tess eyed Stacy suspiciously. "Do you have a replacement in mind already?"

"No, Tess!" Stacy's voice rose. "How cold-blooded do you think I am?" Then, not giving Tess a chance to say something she'd regret, she added, "Besides, there are other things in the world besides boys."

Gina Damone, who was seated next to Tess, nodded in agreement. "Having a boyfriend's not everything, Tess."

Stacy smiled at Gina's naive support. Gina's parents were so strict that they hadn't allowed her to date until now, her senior year. Any girl who'd actually had to attend her own junior prom with some friend of the family couldn't admit boyfriends were important. And Stacy had noticed the hopeful little quaver in Gina's usually lilting voice. Now that she was being allowed to date, boys were so used to not bothering to ask the poor girl out that she still spent her nights at home.

Poor Gina must be desperate for anybody to ask her anywhere, Stacy thought. She couldn't possibly understand Stacy's boredom. Aloud, Stacy said only, "I'd rather be a wallflower than go out with a boy for the wrong reasons."

"Come off it, Stacy," Tess said bluntly.

"Aren't you the one who told me over and over again how important it is to be involved with the right guy? Am I talking to the same Stacy Harcourt who was so excited the first time Dave asked me out?"

"Well, yes," Stacy admitted. "But it's not the same."

"Not the same as what? Oh, I get it. You meant it was important for *me* to get the right guy. Because I'm in a vocational-technical program and techies need all the help they can get to be popular, right?"

"Oh, don't be so paranoid!" Stacy said tartly, even though Tess had been voicing Stacy's exact feelings on the matter. "Any girl Dave Prentice wants to date is lucky. And you haven't turned him down once, have you? It's got nothing to do with your being a vo-tech student."

"Good." Tess smiled smugly. "I'm glad you feel that way. Remind me to remind you of what you just said in case I ever decide to stop going out with Dave and start seeing somebody else."

"Don't be silly. You'd never dream of turning Dave down," Stacy said matter-of-factly. Then, seeing the gleam in Tess's eyes, her voice rose. "Would you?"

Tess shrugged. "You never know. The guy who's been working on my car lately isn't half bad. In fact, you could even say he's quite a hunk."

Gina looked interested, but Stacy's disgusted snort put an end to any more discussion on the subject. "That's too absurd! No girl in her right mind would consider giving up Dave Prentice for some—some grease monkey! And don't think you can rip off my cherry pie while you've got me distracted, sweetie! Keep your fork on your own side of the table."

"C'mon, give me a break! I was just going to take one teensy little bite. Besides, you told me just last week how thin I was looking."

"I said thinner, not thin," Stacy corrected her. Then, seeing how Tess's face had fallen at the remark, she added, "You do look great, Tess, the best you've looked since I've known you. You're the one who's always moaning and groaning about your weight." She grabbed her pie plate, pulling it out of Tess's reach. "I'm just trying to protect you from yourself."

"Boy, now I know what they mean by the saying, 'With friends like you, who needs enemies?'"

All three girls laughed at that, and the conversation turned to the only topic that could seriously compete with boys for their interest— cheering. The first football game of the season was the following weekend. It was a big event for the entire school, but especially for the senior cheerleaders. All three had been on the squad the year before, so cheering was not new to them, but this year they would occupy the spotlight at games, pep rallies, and school social functions.

The seniors really led the cheers. In line formations, they'd be in the center, with the juniors on the sides. In any cheer that called for two rows, the senior girls cheered in the front. And tradition ordered that only the three senior members be considered for election to squad captain for basketball and baseball seasons. The current crop of juniors wouldn't be in the running for any of the three yearly captaincies until the end of the year, when next year's football-squad captain was chosen.

"Speaking of cheering, I'd better get going," Gina announced, standing up and reaching for her tray.

"How come?" Stacy asked. "We don't have practice till Monday."

"Oh, I just—" A deep blush rose up Gina's olive skin and across her cheekbones, and she ducked her head shyly. "I just thought I'd go to the gym and get in some extra practicing on my own."

"Get her!" Stacy said in surprise when Gina had gone. "The best cheerleader on the squad and she's worried about getting in some extra practice. Now, that's what I call dedication."

"Well, there'll be more tryouts eventually," Tess said, looking away as if the sight of Stacy gobbling down the last bite of her cherry pie was too painful to watch.

"Tryouts? Oh, for the basketball season cheering captain? They're not for months yet. Why practice now?"

Stacy didn't add that she thought Gina was wasting her time practicing in the first place, since she herself undoubtedly had the election sewn up. Stacy was willing to admit she couldn't perform better than Gina. But Gina was so standoffish she had no chance of being chosen as captain. The captain had to be best all-around, like Stacy herself. And with her strict parents, Gina could never play center stage, even if she wanted to.

Tess sighed. "My cheering's not bad, but I'd better start studying right now if I want to stay on the squad. Oh, why did I ever decide to take French in the first place?"

"Because you don't want to be just any sort of secretary when you graduate, you want to go to a good business school—like Winston—and be a bilingual secretary and get a glamorous job," Stacy told her friend supportively. "Don't let it get you down, Tess." She reached across the table and patted the other girl's hand. Tess really was having a hard time with her language course. She wasn't just giving in to her well-known tendency to overdramatize her life. "One of these days you'll be *parlez-vous*-ing just like a native. You'll see."

"I hope so." Tess didn't sound very optimistic. "I don't see how I could try any harder. I'm already cutting myself back to one night out a weekend so I can spend the other night hitting the books."

"Even when there's a game and you've got to cheer one night?"

"Even when there's a game. You don't know how lucky you are, Stacy. Everything's a breeze for you. Sometimes I feel like I've got to work so hard to get anything I want."

"Stop putting yourself down, Tess," Stacy said firmly. "You never give yourself enough credit. Honestly, I've never known anyone so hooked on self-improvement." She smiled warmly at her best friend, who had been cute and cuddly and friendly as a puppy since the day they met across the table in kindergarten. "You know, you don't have to buy *Cosmo* every month and experiment with every new makeup and hairstyle that comes along to be popular. Brooke Shields doesn't even pluck her eyebrows. Everyone at Midvale adores you just for yourself."

As if Stacy's words had conjured up a demon, Valerie Masters picked just that moment to strut by, crossing with a tray from the cafeteria line to the other side of the lunchroom, where the majorettes had their own table.

"Don't worry, Tess, honey," Valerie drawled, her pale blue eyes cold as ice. "The frizz on that new perm will grow out in no time." With a superior smile, she flicked her long honey-colored braid over one shoulder, gave Stacy a warm hello, then continued across the room.

"There's a perfect example of adoration!"

Tess snorted. "Can't you tell Valerie's just dying for me to be her new best friend?"

"Come on, you know better than to take Valerie seriously, don't you?" Stacy said, making it more of a statement than a question. She'd lost count of the times she'd tried to convince Tess not to take Valerie's snubs so personally. Being a majorette wasn't quite enough for Valerie; she longed to claim the captain of the cheering squad as one of her clique. And in Valerie's all-too-simple view of things, Tess was the barrier keeping her from Stacy. It amazed Stacy that Val hadn't seen the simple truth by now: the more she tried to torture Tess with cruel remarks, the more Stacy avoided her. She was friendly to Valerie, as she was to everyone, but she made it clear she had no interest in becoming part of the gaggle of girls Val led through the halls of Midvale.

"Oh, Valerie takes herself seriously enough for all of us," Tess agreed, but she didn't sound entirely convinced. "I just wish she hadn't convinced Joanie Gregson not to invite me to her party next week."

"Well, you know how Joanie is. She'll do anything Valerie says. Look, you're not mad at me for saying I'll go, are you?" Stacy asked. "If you are, I'll stay away."

"Of course not, Stace. You know I'm not like that. Besides, if I'm going out after the game Saturday, I couldn't go out Friday night, too. My one-night-a-weekend rule, remember?"

"Well, it's probably good for me to start going to parties by myself, anyhow. I'd better get used to being an old maid."

"You really kill me!" Tess laughed. "Once the word gets around that you're not seeing Rich, every guy in town will be asking you out. At least every guy who's not too intimidated to have the nerve."

"You think so?" Stacy asked uncertainly. Then she stood up. "Come on, let's hit the girls' room before next period. If I don't do something about my face, I'll look like death warmed over, and boys will be running for their lives instead of asking me out."

A deep male voice interrupted their laughter.

Both girls looked up to see Dex Grantham standing a few feet from them, balancing a tray on one hand while extending the other in a sweeping gesture that went with his low bow. He turned toward Stacy, one dark eyebrow cocked, to give her the full benefit of his smile and his perfectly straight white teeth. "I'm absolutely stunned by the hot gossip that you've finally come to your senses and realized there are better men in this world than Rich Stinson. Is it true?"

"It's true I'm not seeing Rich anymore," Stacy replied. "As to whether there are better men in the world"—she smiled and fluttered her eyelashes in a Scarlett O'Hara imitation—"that remains to be seen."

Dex pulled himself up to his full five foot ten, preening from the tips of his penny loafers to the collar of his polo shirt. "I know you cheerleaders think the only sports that matter are the big three, namely football, basketball, and baseball. But you know we've got a decent swim team—"

"And you're the star," Stacy finished for him.

"You got it, gorgeous. By the way," he added with a joking leer, "if you manage to improve your backhand, I might even give you a game at the club one of these weekends."

Tess laughed. "He's all heart, isn't he, Stace?" To Dex, she said, "You know darned well Stacy's the best tennis player in the school and could whip the pants off you any day."

"Oh, if only you would!" he begged, his leer growing so blatant that Stacy blushed in spite of her laughter.

"I'll pass on that. All those spoiled rich kids at the club give me a pain."

"Present company excepted, of course," Dex reminded her. "After all, it's not my fault I have to tool around in a Porsche, is it?"

"Poor thing!" Stacy said coolly, knowing Dex's father, who was one of the best surgeons in the state, gave Dex anything he wanted. "It's a rough life, isn't—"

But before she could finish what she was about to say, Valerie's strident voice rang in her ears. "Dex! Come sit with us for a minute! I want to talk to you!"

"What can I say?" Dex asked as he turned away. "It's not easy always being in demand."

"How can any guy be so stuck-up?" Stacy asked as she and Tess handed in their trays at the dishwashing window. "He always tries to act like he's just kidding, but the boy's got a real case on himself."

"At least he admits he's a creep," Tess said mildly. "You know, I'll bet if Valerie hadn't screeched like that, he'd have asked you out."

"You think so?" Stacy's eyes lit up. Then she shook her head. "What am I saying? I don't want to go out with a snob like Dex Grantham even if he is great-looking. You just wait. I'm going to be living proof that a girl can have a terrific time without a boyfriend. You'll see!"

"Well, if you can't do it, no one can," Tess said admiringly.

"Come on, let's get to the girls' room before there's such a mob you can't see yourself in the mirror. I don't want to show up in class looking so bad that everyone thinks I'm a free woman these days 'cause nobody wants me."

"You wouldn't even say something like that if you weren't sure you could get any guy you wanted," Tess told her as they walked out into the corridor.

"The trouble is, there's nobody I do want right now, and maybe there never will be," Stacy said. And she meant it.

THREE

"Are you sure you don't mind?" Tess asked the following Monday as she opened the passenger door of the little Honda that had been handed down to Stacy when Sarah had driven off to college in a brand-new model. "I can always take the bus, you know."

"Don't be silly. Of course I don't mind," Stacy insisted as she fastened her seat belt and turned the key in the ignition. "Cooper's Garage, over on the highway, right? Past the Dairy Bar?"

"Right. It should be ready." Tess checked her watch. "They said by three-thirty, and it's almost five. Good practice, wasn't it?"

"Uh-huh," Stacy replied absently and carefully guided the car onto the road, where a stream of rush-hour traffic was already starting to flow out of Midvale's small business district.

"I loved the new jazzy routine Gina worked up," Tess went on. "What do you think, though?

Will the juniors be able to get it down by Saturday?"

"Sherri can do it already. She's a natural, like Gina. I suppose if Kathy and Pixie keep their word and practice, they'll be fine."

"Patricia."

"What about Patricia?" Stacy stopped at an intersection and momentarily took her eyes off the road to glance sideways.

"Pixie wants to be called Patricia from now on, remember? She's decided she doesn't want to have a nickname that reminds everyone she's barely five feet tall."

"Whoops! And I forgot already. Maybe we should add name practice to cheering practice," Stacy remarked. It was like Tess to remember something like that, something that had left Stacy's mind the instant after Pixie—no, Patricia—made her request. Tess was naturally thoughtful, but Stacy knew it was one of the things she had to work at sometimes.

Now, as if to show how thoughtful she truly was, Tess said again, "Are you sure you don't mind? It's not as if the garage is on your way home."

"You know I wouldn't do it if I minded," Stacy told her. "Besides—"

"Besides what?" Tess asked as her friend's voice faded.

"Besides, Daddy had a trial today, so we won't be having dinner until seven or later."

"I wish my father did something exciting

30

like being a lawyer," Tess said wistfully. "Being an accountant seems like such a dull occupation."

Stacy murmured a noncommittal "Mm-hmm," but she wasn't really listening as Tess chattered about not understanding how her dad could be a whiz with numbers while she had trouble adding two and two. Stacy was thinking about what she'd almost blurted out a moment before. Tess wouldn't have understood if she'd actually said, "Besides, I've got nothing to do at home and I'm so bored I could scream."

Tess would have been mystified by Stacy's claim. Stacy had an expensive stereo and a color TV and a VCR and a computer complete with games. The Harcourts had a housekeeper to do the chores. They lived in one of the most magnificent houses in Midvale. Stacy had been born lucky. The funny thing was, she knew it. She had no solid reason for the feeling that kept coming over her lately, the feeling that her life left a whole lot to be desired. But she couldn't help it. It was there, nudging her all the time, making her restless, itchy.

She had another reason for offering to drive Tess to the garage to pick up her VW bug with its brand-new muffler. But she'd never confess her second reason, either.

Stacy wanted to visit the mechanic who worked on Tess's car and make sure he got the picture, that he understood Tess wasn't available, that she and Dave Prentice were almost serious.

The least she could do as Tess's friend was save her from ruining her whole senior year by getting involved with a mechanic. She knew Tess was sensitive about the subject, but the truth was that a girl who wanted to be a secretary in a school where the in-crowd went to college and took only academic classes couldn't afford to let someone like Dave Prentice slip through her fingers. Certainly not for a guy who spent his day covered with grease and had probably dropped out of school in the eighth grade.

"Gum?" Tess broke into Stacy's thoughts, holding out a pack.

"Ugh! You know what a disgusting habit I think that is." Stacy wrinkled her nose.

"I know, I know." Without taking a stick herself, Tess slipped the pack back into her clutch purse. "Especially when someone cracks it the way I do. You must think I'm so L.C., Stacy! But sometimes I just forget."

The abbreviation *L.C.* was one of Stacy's favorites. It stood for "low class," and she applied it to anything that didn't meet with her approval.

"Do you think I'd be your friend if I thought you were L.C.?" she asked Tess. "I just think you're too classy to do things like chew gum."

Tess, whose high spirits could never stay dampened for long, laughed. "You know, you sound just like my mom when you say things like that. 'You're a beautiful girl, Tess, you don't need all that eye makeup,'" she said in an imitation of her mother's gentle tones.

"Do I really get on your case that much?" Stacy chuckled. "I promise to be less of a nag. Anyhow, you know your mom means well. And she's less like a mother than any other mother I know. I mean, can you see my mother in a pair of jeans and a sweatshirt?"

"If I didn't know you, Stacy, I'd swear families like yours just existed in TV series," Tess admitted. "I sure can't imagine your mom and dad ever screaming and yelling at each other."

"They don't," Stacy said. "Gosh, wouldn't it be awful to have parents who were fighting all the time?"

"Mine only fight half the time, and that's bad enough," Tess said quietly.

"Oh, I'm sure mine must argue more than they let on," Stacy said brightly, more to reassure Tess that other adults bickered the way Tess's parents had in Stacy's presence than because she thought her parents actually raised their voices at each other. "They always say you can't love someone if you don't fight with them. Maybe that was the trouble with me and Rich," she added. "We never had a real fight. I guess we didn't care enough to fight."

"If that's caring, I'll take indifference," Tess insisted. "You turn right at the next light and go in the side entrance. I hope this is my last car repair for a while. My dad says he's tired of shelling out money to keep that clunker going, so the next time it goes, I guess I'll be carless forever."

"Live without a car!" Stacy's voice was practically a shriek. "That would be impossible."

"Really, Stacy, lots of kids don't have their own cars," Tess informed her.

"Well, sure, I know that," Stacy agreed. But she didn't manage to sound convincing. "Where are the gas pumps at this place?" she asked as she pulled the car around to the side.

"It's not that sort of garage. They just do repair work here. I think that's Nick over there." She pointed to a mechanic whose top half was hidden as he bent over a car. "Uh-oh!"

"What's wrong?" Stacy asked, her gaze following Tess's finger. "Are you afraid he's stealing something from the trunk?"

"Of course not. Nick Cooper's not that kind of guy. Anyway, I've got a VW, remember? That's not the trunk—it's the hood. I don't know what in the world I'll do if he's found something else wrong!"

She hurried over, while Stacy followed at a slower pace. "What's wrong, Nick?" Tess asked nervously as she approached the car.

"Nothing, Tess," Stacy heard a husky male voice say. "I was just wiping off your battery. You should try to do a little more maintenance yourself. If you do, this car's going to run forever."

Well, at least the jerk isn't trying to rip poor Tess off by charging her for a bunch of repairs she doesn't need, Stacy thought with relief. Then the figure working beneath the hood stood up, and Stacy couldn't think anymore. All she could do was stare.

Nick Cooper was the most handsome boy she'd ever seen. Not only the most handsome, but the sexiest. He was just plain gorgeous, from his square jaw to his thick, tousled chestnut hair.

He was every movie star and rock singer she'd ever had a crush on, every sports star and TV idol, all combined in one breathtaking boy, she decided, unable to tear her eyes away from him.

As Nick started explaining some little things Tess could do to the car on her own, Stacy stood spellbound, her eyes taking in every inch of his rugged good looks and muscular body. The black twill coveralls he wore did nothing to hide the strength and power of his sinewy arms and long legs. She felt almost faint when he stretched slightly and his broad shoulders strained against the fabric.

Everything Stacy had ever said or thought about the right kind of boy abandoned her as Nick lifted a grimy hand to push a lock of hair away from eyes that were the rich, warm brown of bittersweet chocolate and were framed by a long fringe of dark lashes. *This guy's got charisma*, she thought weakly. If only there was a chance of finding anyone with those looks and that magnetism at Midvale High!

She was still staring when Nick looked straight up into her eyes.

From far, far away, she heard Tess saying, "Stacy, this is Nick Cooper. Nick, Stacy Harcourt."

A dimple deepened to the right of his mouth as it spread in a smile, revealing teeth so white and straight they eclipsed even Dex Grantham's. "Oh, I know who Stacy is," he said in a voice so low and heavy it sent a shiver up Stacy's spine.

"You do?" Stacy, who never blushed, reddened as she heard the feeble croak that was her voice.

"Of course. Doesn't everyone at Midvale High School know who Stacy Harcourt is?" he asked, his grin crooked and teasing now.

Before she could think, Stacy heard the words rushing from her mouth. "But you don't mean you go to Midvale? That's impossible! I thought I knew everyone there."

"Everyone who doesn't take vo-tech classes, right?" he asked.

Mortified by her blunder, Stacy gulped and searched in a panic for the right words. "That's not true," she finally managed to blurt. "Tess is in vo-tech and she's my best friend!"

The look Tess gave her made her blush even more deeply. The tips of her earlobes were on fire.

"Touché," Nick said in amusement, and his low chuckle told her he wasn't the least bit bothered. *Funny*, Stacy thought as Nick turned back to Tess, explaining more details about car maintenance, *he's really proud of being a techie.*

Twilight was settling. Inside the garage, someone flipped a switch, bathing the asphalt work-area where the three stood in a yellow glare. Even under that harsh light, Nick looked as handsome as a Greek god carved in marble, like a picture from one of the art books on Stacy's parents' coffee table.

"Let me know if you have any more trouble," Nick told Tess as he folded her check and slipped it in a pocket of his coveralls. "But it should be fine now."

"You made my day," Tess assured him. "I feel a hundred percent better just knowing the old heap's going to go a few more miles. Thanks, Nick."

"Sure, Tess. Any time." He smiled, a smile that widened to include Stacy. "See you around," he said lightly, then added, with a taunting wink, "even if you don't see me."

Stacy's cheeks began to burn again, and she chided herself for acting like such an obvious fool.

"What's the big idea, Stace?" her friend asked acidly as they drove away from the garage. " 'Tess is in vo-tech,' " she mimicked, her voice dripping with saccharine sweetness. "I thought you just shriveled up with shame and wanted to die whenever anyone discovered you hung around with a techie! Or have you already forgotten how much energy you wasted sophomore year trying to convince me to switch out of my typing and shorthand classes?"

"You know I got over that long ago," Stacy protested. "I mean, it's not as if you hang out with those yucky guys in motorcycle boots and gold earrings. Anyway, how can Nick be a Midvale student and have this kind of job, too?"

"He doesn't work full time. Just after school and on Saturdays. His uncle owns the place and is going to make Nick a partner in the business after graduation."

"Well, you should have told me the great Nick Cooper went to school with us, for crying out loud! You should realize how awful it was, a cheerleader not even *recognizing* someone from her own class. I was just trying to make the poor guy feel less out of it. That's the only reason I said that stuff."

Tess shot her a look of disbelief. "Come on, Stace, with hundreds of kids in each class, I can't see how anyone's expected to know every senior. Besides, I think Nick is perfectly happy in vo-tech, probably more than I am. He hangs out with other techies who like to work on cars the way he does. If you asked him, he'd probably tell you I'm nuts for wanting to hang out with kids who take classes like calculus and physics and worry about getting into a good college."

"Don't be ridiculous. It's our crowd, Tess,

yours *and* mine. Just because the other kids aren't in vo-tech is no reason to be so paranoid. Anyhow," she added, looking slightly alarmed as she pulled into the driveway of the Beldings' small brick ranch house, "you're not planning to go totally techie, are you? Promise you won't show up at school tomorrow in a tube top, skintight jeans, and platform heels, okay?"

"I promise." Tess snorted at the idea. "I may not be the world's greatest dresser, but I'm not that bad! And you may not realize it, Stacy, but not all the kids in vo-tech are uncivilized goons or greasers or punkers or sleazeballs. You obviously didn't think Nick was like that, did you?"

"Noooo," Stacy agreed slowly. "I know you must think I'm a terrible snob, Tess. But I don't think Nick's in Dave Prentice's league. You'd be silly to give up Dave to get involved with him."

"Who said I'm getting involved with him?" Tess asked, wide-eyed. "All I ever did was say the guy was great-looking, Stacy. It's not as if he's ever asked me out or anything."

"Oh, of course not," Stacy said quickly. "I didn't mean I thought you were actually interested in him."

But what if Tess really is interested in Nick? Stacy asked herself a few minutes later as she was driving east toward her own house.

It would be a shame if Tess threw away her relationship with Dave. Much as she insisted Tess's being in vo-tech didn't matter, Stacy knew it did count. Sure, Tess was well liked and popular. But that didn't mean she could afford to flout the unspoken rules of Midvale High School.

Not that Stacy would dream of interfering in someone else's life. Still, she resolved to keep a cautious eye on Tess in the days to come.

And she'd better keep an eye on Nick Cooper, too.

FOUR

"You always know what to do, Stacy," Gina Damone said earnestly the next day as the two girls walked out of homeroom. "How can I ever get a date—short of taking out an ad in the school paper? There must be something I can do!"

"Well, I don't think putting a big notice in the *Sentinel* is the answer." Stacy smiled.

"I probably won't have a boyfriend till I'm sixty-five!" Gina wailed. "It would serve my folks right if I end up an old maid and they're stuck with me forever."

"It's really a bummer, their being so strict," Stacy said sympathetically, seeing the fear and frustration in Gina's big dark eyes. She could imagine how Gina must feel. After all, Stacy had just broken off with Rich a week ago, and even she was worried in her weak moments that she would never date another boy.

"Maybe it's just me. Maybe I'm just so weird-looking, nobody even wants a date!"

"C'mon, you're not the slightest bit weird-looking!" Stacy insisted. She had often admired Gina's quiet dark looks. "You don't know how lucky you are to be so exotic instead of a bland blond like me."

"Bland!" Gina's soft, husky voice was a single syllable of disbelief. "I'd give anything to be a bland blond—like Christie Brinkley and Jessica Lange. Look at me, Stacy," she insisted, sounding miserable. "My skin's so olive it's almost green, and my hair's black—that's as far from blond as you can get. How can you complain about being peaches and cream when I look like something you'd find in an antipasto?"

"The day you look like an olive is the day Sophia Loren looks like a submarine sandwich," Stacy teased, trying to kid Gina out of the doldrums. "So you don't look like every other cornfed midwesterner, so what? You've got a great figure, you're a terrific dancer, and you're unique as well as pretty. What's so bad about that?"

"Something must be," Gina retorted. "Otherwise, where are all the boys hiding?"

"Well, you've just got to make a real effort to make sure everybody knows you're available," Stacy suggested.

Just then the first bell went off, and she spied Nick Cooper lounging against the wall by a row of lockers, talking to two other guys who had that unmistakable vo-tech look. Somehow Nick stood apart, even though he wore black boots, black chinos, and a T-shirt like the others. Stacy found it hard to believe she hadn't noticed him before.

"Look," she said to Gina, "I see somebody I've got to talk to. You go on to chem, and I'll see you there."

"It's only three minutes to the late bell," Gina reminded her. "You know how Mr. Peabody is about lateness."

"Don't worry, I'll make it," Stacy assured her, already hurrying to where Nick and his buddies stood.

"Hi, Nick," she said brightly. "I was hoping I'd see you today."

"Oh, yeah? Uh, what's up, Stacy?" he asked, sounding so nervous that Stacy was momentarily speechless. Hadn't he all but flirted with her only the day before?

But it was too late to ignore him now. Turning her back as much as possible on the other guys, she explained, "Well, see, I noticed this, um, this funny squeak under the hood of my car when I was driving to school, and, well, Tess was telling me how good you are with your hands—oh, I mean, she was saying you knew everything about cars and that you were so much better than her boyfriend when it came to fixing things and figuring out what was wrong that—" She cut her words off abruptly as she realized she was babbling and that Nick was looking away. Why, it was almost as if *he* were embarrassed to be seen talking to *her*.

"Look, why don't you jot down your number on a piece of paper?" he said, clipping his syllables as if to let her know she was embarrassing him. "I'll have to give you a call from the garage to let you know the best time to bring it in."

"Oh, uh, okay. Sure, I'll do that." She pawed frantically through her purse, trying not to drop her books before she could locate a pen and get away from there.

"Here, just tell it to me."

She looked up to see Nick waiting with a pencil, and as she quickly reeled off her number, he scrawled it on the inside of a book titled *Basic Engine Rebuilding*. With a muttered goodbye, she turned and hurried back down the hallway, thinking it would serve her right if she got in trouble with Mr. Peabody, risking tardiness just to be nice to a creep like Nick Cooper.

Well, it's not as if I did it because I like him or anything like that, Stacy thought as she raced down the corridor and slid breathlessly into an empty seat at a lab desk just as the final bell started clanging.

She'd never have given someone like Nick more than a brief hello if she hadn't been trying to protect her best friend. *At least I accomplished that*, she thought. Now Nick knew Tess had a boyfriend and wasn't interested in him. Not that Dave Prentice was really her boyfriend yet—but he never would be if Tess had foolish notions about going out with a boy like Nick.

He was obviously a creep—like those friends of his. She'd heard them all chortling as she rushed away, heard one of those animals croon, "Oh, Nickie, you're sooo good with your hands." Just remembering the whole thing, Stacy trembled with anger.

The rest of the day was tainted by her bad experience with Nick, starting with Mr. Peabody drawling in that bored, superior way of his when she hadn't even heard him call on her in class, "I know chemistry isn't the most exciting subject on earth for everyone, Ms. Harcourt, but I can't give you a grade based on daydreaming." Her face had burned at the muffled giggles of her classmates.

On the way to the cafeteria, she almost bumped into none other than Rich Stinson walking along the hall with Kathy Phillips, the junior cheerleader who looked enough like Stacy to be her younger sister. Neither of them even noticed her, which was just as well. The expression on her face couldn't have been very pleasant, not with the way Rich was all but drooling over the girl she recalled his once dismissing as "a poor imitation of the real thing."

The lunch special was Stacy's least favorite food in the whole world—macaroni drowning in cheese sauce that was too bright an orange to be real and that tasted like paste. Neither Tess nor Gina was at lunch. Both had brown-bagged it so they could use the time to practice cheering. When they'd told her of their plan at practice the day before, she'd thought they were both wasting their time, since they were already on the squad and everyone knew Stacy would certainly continue as captain for the whole school year. Now she almost wished she'd followed their example. She ended up sitting with Valerie's crowd and listening to the same catty remarks her clique was always making.

By the time the last bell of the day rang, she couldn't wait to get to her car. As she raced out of the parking lot, she heard the engine purring smoothly and vaguely wondered what had happened to the squeak she'd heard that morning. She was sure she had heard one. Not that it mattered, she realized, since she didn't plan to exchange another word with Nick Cooper as long as she lived.

Coming home to the pristine quietness of the big house brought no relief. Emma was in the kitchen larding a roast, too busy preparing dinner to have much to say to Stacy except that Mrs. Harcourt had gone straight to the hairdresser's from her garden club meeting.

Today, even the bedroom she so loved seemed like a prison—well furnished but confining, nevertheless. Stacy put her favorite old Bayside Boys album on the turntable, but even the melodies that filled the room seemed flat and meaningless.

Her two tennis rackets lay in their cases, propped against the wall below the big poster of Bjorn Borg that dominated the room. Once, she remembered, a few sets of tennis were all that it took to banish the blues. But she hadn't played much since Sarah had left for college. It always seemed like too much trouble trying to round up a partner. *Maybe I should take Dex Grantham up on his offer and stop by the country club sometime over the weekend*, she thought. She couldn't continue sitting around in a funk by herself.

The telephone rang as she flipped idly through the pages of the latest *Glamour*, and she reached for it without enthusiasm. It was probably Tess, wondering why Stacy had slipped off so suddenly after school.

Her heart fluttered with anticipation when a hesitant male voice asked, "Hi, is this Stacy?" A call from a boy—any boy—was better than looking at the magazine pages she had practically memorized in her boredom.

"Yes, this is Stacy," she answered. "Can you hang on a sec while I turn down the stereo?" When she'd resettled herself on the bed, she picked up the receiver again and said, "Okay, now I can hear you."

"Hey, Stacy, it's Nick Cooper."

"Oh, hi," she said as flatly as possible. He'd probably called to tell her when she could bring in her car. Big deal.

She was about to tell him she hadn't heard that funny squeak again and to forget the whole thing when he said, "Look, I wanted to tell you I was sorry if I seemed sort of rude in the hall today. You know how those guys are." Then, as if realizing that someone like Stacy might not be all that familiar with the actions and attitudes of his friends, he added, "Hey, they'd never have let me live it down if they'd caught me gushing all over some cheerleader."

Stacy's heart began to beat a little faster. "Oh, that's all right, Nick. I wasn't mad or anything," she lied. "I guess I shouldn't have bothered you with business at school, anyhow."

"No, no," he said quickly. "That's okay, honest. I'd be real glad to take a look under the hood for you. You can bring the car over right now if you want."

The squeak might reappear at any moment. Stacy almost said she'd be right over, when she caught herself. Just in time, too. After all, Stacy Harcourt wasn't the kind of girl who came running, no matter what boy snapped his fingers.

Instead, she said, "Gee, that's nice of you, Nick, but I'm tied up now." She bit back a giggle as she winked at Bjorn, who watched her with a smile from the wall across from the bed. "Maybe tomorrow after cheering practice."

"You mean the same time you and Tess came by yesterday? That'd be good."

"That's fine, then," she said. "I'll see you tomorrow."

She hung up and crossed the room to flip over the album on the turntable. The music didn't seem boring anymore. Her life wasn't so flat and eventless. And to think that just a few minutes before she actually had been considering asking Dex Grantham to play tennis with her!

Of course, she told herself, *it's not as if I'm actually interested in Nick Cooper.* But she couldn't help feeling better now that he'd realized his mistake and gone out of his way to apologize. She wouldn't dream of going out of her way to impress any boy.

She sang loudly along with the Bayside Boys and managed a few tricky dance steps as she made her way over to the big walk-in closet in the corner. Now was as good a time as any to put together an eye-stopping outfit to wear to school the following day.

FIVE

The next day's practice was a good one. It was pretty easy for Stacy as captain; this early in the season, all the girls were full of energy. The juniors needed the most attention, since many of the cheers were new for them, though the routines weren't too demanding for Patricia and Sherri, who'd been on the J.V. squad.

Stacy firmly pushed any thoughts of Cooper's Garage out of her mind as she carefully worked with Ms. Bowen to oversee the practice session. The entire squad was her responsibility. Ms. Bowen made suggestions and coached on jumps and timing, but in the end, it was Stacy who had to make sure nothing went wrong.

Today, she used her power to veto one of the two new cheers for the upcoming game. When she announced that she wasn't happy with it, groans mingled with sighs of relief. "But it's such a neat cheer!" Sherri, the most outspoken of the juniors, protested. "Isn't it supposed to replace that boring old 'You can't tame the Mustangs' thing?"

"That's right." Stacy nodded. "Only we're all good at doing that boring old *thing*, as you put it. And I don't think we've got this new cheer down pat yet." As Sherri continued to protest, Stacy cut her off. "You've got to remember that you and Gina have an easier time with the jumps than the rest of us, Sherri. It still needs some work. We'll do it when everybody looks as expert as you do."

Sherri smiled and nodded in agreement.

That's the challenge of being captain, Stacy thought. It took a special sort of tact and diplomacy to lay down the law without rubbing anyone the wrong way. She'd managed to flatter Sherri without giving in to her. If she had folded, the girls who were having a hard time with the cheer—mainly Tess and Kathy—would have held it against her. Instead, everyone was happy.

"Good practice," the three juniors chimed in unison as they hurried out of the dressing room afterward, not bothering to change from their practice clothes. "See you at Nicola's."

"Boy, am I glad you knocked out that new cheer," Tess said as she struggled to slip into her snug black jeans. "One new routine's more than enough for me to remember."

"I'll be glad to help you with the jumps," Gina offered, looking up from her locker as she stashed her practice outfit. "They're not so bad once you've memorized the order of them and don't have to think so much."

"I'd definitely appreciate all the help I can get," Tess assured her. Turning to Stacy, who was seated on the bench, still untying her blue tennis shoes, she asked, "How come you're poking around so much? There'll be no booths left at the pizza parlor by the time we get there."

"Oh, I should have told you." Stacy looked up. "I can't go to Nicola's today. I promised my mother I'd go to the market for her on the way home."

"You're doing grocery shopping?" Grinning, Tess shook her head. "You never fail to amaze me, I swear. Well, if you get done in time, come by, okay? Come on, Gina, you can go in my car."

Stacy breathed more easily when they'd left and she was all alone, taking her time repairing her makeup and brushing her hair until it glistened. She felt almost criminal, fibbing to Tess about going to the market. But she thought it was better not to mention Nick Cooper, since the less Tess thought about him, the stronger her chances were of keeping her eyes only on Dave.

When Stacy pulled into Cooper's, Nick came hurrying over to the car. In his coveralls, with "Nick" embroidered on the breast and "Cooper's Garage" emblazoned in deep red across the back, he again appeared self-assured and powerful.

"Let's have a look," he said confidently after Stacy had unlatched the hood lock and slipped out of the car. Slapping a metallic blue front fender, he told her, "One thing about these Hondas. You'll never have to worry about paying an arm and a leg for repairs. They're kid's play to work on."

Then he ducked under the hood, but not before his velvety brown eyes surveyed Stacy from head to toe, gleaming with approval at her fawn cords and tweed blazer, an outfit she knew set off her blond hair and made her look sophisticated and collegiate.

She was dismayed to find Nick all business at first, asking her to get back in the driver's seat and rev the motor while he tinkered with a wrench someplace in the vicinity of the engine.

When he finally emerged, he was shaking his head and ruffling his curly hair. "Looks all right to me," he said, his attitude professional. "Can't imagine what could have been squeaking. The belts look pretty new and your carburetor's clean as a whistle. The idle was a little high, so I set it down a bit. It won't run so fast now."

As Stacy climbed back out of the car, Nick pushed down on the front bumper with all his strength. Stacy could see once again the muscles tensing in his tanned forearms, the rippling of the cloth around his biceps. "Nope. Shock absorbers seem all right." He grinned. "Looks like you've got yourself a pretty together set of wheels here."

Stacy felt suddenly disappointed, though she couldn't figure out why. Shouldn't she be glad there was nothing seriously the matter with her car, that the squeak seemed to have been nothing more than a figment of her imagination? Or was she just disappointed because Nick had slammed the hood closed and was brushing off his hands in what could have been dismissal?

"No charge for that," he said with a smile, and Stacy might have thought he was flirting if he hadn't added, "since I didn't really do anything at all."

"You sure do know a lot about cars," she said, unwilling to let the encounter end but wishing she could think of something more interesting to say. After all, she didn't want the poor guy to think she was a snob.

Still, she knew she had said the right thing by the way Nick's handsome face lit up with pleasure. "They're just machines," he said modestly. "You work on enough of them, you get to know the quirks of different makes and models."

She just nodded, wondering what she could say next. Other than the location of the gas tank and the proper air pressure for the tires, Stacy knew next to nothing about automobiles. She might as well have been trying to discuss nuclear physics with Gina Damone's father, who was a professor of engineering at one of the state colleges.

"I'm a total dummy about cars," she finally admitted. "Would you believe I didn't know a

Volkswagen's engine was in the back until the other day?"

She laughed, and he joined in. "I'm sure you know about a lot of stuff that's Greek to me," he admitted, and from the way he leaned against her car she could tell he didn't want her to hurry off.

"Are you going to the game Saturday?" she asked.

"Naw, I've got to work. The only games I get to see are the night games, since I'm here working every day after school till we close at eight, and I start at ten in the morning Saturdays."

"Don't you mind that?" she asked curiously. "Working all day Saturday?"

"Not really. The time goes pretty fast. And my uncle Joe works on his own from seven-thirty until I come in, so at least I can sleep later than during the week. I'm usually pretty beat by then, since I hang out at the Grove lots of Friday nights."

"The Grove?" Stacy perked up. Was it possible there was a new club or disco in Midvale she hadn't discovered?

"Sure, Watson's Grove," he said. When Stacy shook her head uncomprehendingly, his eyebrows raised in amazement. "You mean to say you've lived here all your life and have never gone to Watson's Grove Speedway? Hey, people come from all over the state, even from Ohio and Michigan, to go to the stocks and drags there." He heard the enthusiasm in his own voice and chuckled. "Listen to me, mouthing off about stock-car races to a girl like you! I'll bet you spend every weekend night at the Hay Loft or the Rumpus Room or some other club."

"I used to," Stacy admitted. Then, looking away from him, she took a deep breath and went on, "Of course, since I broke up with Rich Stinson, I really haven't been doing much of anything. . . ."

"No?"

Stacy just shook her head, holding her breath during the long pause that followed. Finally, Nick said slowly, "Well, look, I, uh, I promised a buddy of mine I'd work the pit for him during Friday's races, but if you're not busy after the game Saturday, maybe we could catch a movie or something."

She looked up to see that Nick was avoiding her eyes just as she'd avoided his. *Why, he's actually shy with me,* she thought with pleasure. It was hard to imagine someone with Nick Cooper's looks and *presence* being ill at ease with anybody.

A little surge of power made her feel light-headed, and she thought, *Why not? What harm could there be in going out with a boy like Nick just one time? Once, she was sure, would be enough.* "That sounds fine," she said.

Nick blinked, as if he couldn't believe he

had heard correctly. Then he grinned. "Should I pick you up at your place after the game?" he asked.

"No, no, I'll come here," she said quickly. "I wasn't planning to stop at home after the game, anyhow."

Saying goodbye, she headed home, wondering if Nick would have looked so flattered by her acceptance if he'd known that nobody had asked her out for so much as a soda since she'd stopped seeing Rich. Tess was probably right when she said plenty of guys were too intimidated to ask Stacy for a date. Still, no dates meant no dates any way Stacy looked at it.

And a date with Nick Cooper won instantly over hanging out with the gang at the pizza parlor after the game. Stacy knew she'd be miserable watching everyone gush over Rich, who was sure to score at least one touchdown during the contest against Brownville. She didn't want him anymore, but neither did she want to sit by, watching while everybody else made a fuss over him.

So she knew she'd done the right thing in accepting Nick's offer. Now the only thing she had to do was tell Tess. After all, Tess had seen him first, though Stacy knew Tess hadn't really been serious about giving up Dave for Nick. And, of course, it wasn't as if she herself were genuinely interested in Nick as a boyfriend. She wasn't even planning to date him more than once. Still, Stacy believed in being honest with her friends. Not that there was any hurry. She had until Saturday to think of the right way to break the news. She pulled into Hawthorne Lane resolving to find the right way to do it before the time came.

No sooner had the heavy front door closed behind her than her mother hurried in from the living room. "I was beginning to think your cheerleading practice would go all night," Emily Harcourt fretted, looking at the delicate gold watch on her slender wrist. "Your father and I have a township meeting right after dinner, you know."

Alexander Harcourt was one of the attorneys who donated time and advice to the local township board, which met one evening a month. Stacy vaguely remembered her mother saying something at breakfast about having an early dinner.

"Sorry, Mother, I got hung up." She tried to sound apologetic, but she couldn't completely erase the smile from her lips. She was too pleased at the way things had gone with Nick to look really regretful. "Daddy home already?"

Mrs. Harcourt nodded, automatically raising one hand to smooth her sleek blond chignon. "He's in the den. I'll get him, dear, if you'll just stop in the kitchen and let Emma know we're ready to eat."

She hurried off with a swish of silk, the sweet scent of her rose-and-jasmine perfume lingering in the air. Stacy dropped her books on the hall table and headed in the opposite direction, through the dining room with its cut-glass chandelier and long oak table, into the kitchen.

Emma's broad back was bent over the range as she stirred first one pot and then another. "Hi, I'm home, and Mother says we're ready to eat now, Emma," Stacy announced. "Can I help with anything?"

Still stirring with one hand, Emma bent down and opened the oven door as she turned toward Stacy. Her wide lined face was flushed from the heat, and her cropped gray hair stuck out in all directions, but she looked calm. Anyone who'd managed to keep the busy Harcourts organized since before either Stacy or Sarah had been born had to have an iron grip on staying cool and collected. "If you'll just grab the bread basket and that dish of peach chutney off the table there, Stacy, I can get the rest," she requested mildly, quickly turning off both burners and the oven.

"Sure, no problem," Stacy said generously, picking up the chutney dish and the basket of bread and carrying them to the dining room, where she plunked them down on the damask cloth.

She never minded helping Emma. Stacy appreciated having live-in help and not being forced to do her own drudge work. Making her own bed in the morning was no trouble. Of course, Emma was the one who actually changed the sheets and vacuumed and dusted—

and tried to cure Stacy of the habit of leaving things scattered all over her bedroom.

"What would I do without you, Emma?" Stacy had asked more than once. "I could never have your knack of organizing things and keeping them clean. I wish I could lend you out to some of my friends for a day or two. You should see *their* rooms!"

"I think I've got my hands full enough with you, dear," Emma would tell her, and for the next few days Stacy would make more of an effort than usual to show her appreciation.

Tonight, Mr. and Mrs. Harcourt were concerned with their meeting, and over the roast and mashed potatoes they discussed a new zoning proposal Alexander Harcourt had been checking out for the board. He was jubilant, and his hazel eyes gleamed behind his horn-rimmed glasses. "I knew there was a statute that would back us up on this one, Emily," he told Stacy's mother. "And it was well worth the weeks it took me to find it. Unless there's a big campaign to change some ordinances, there's no chance of big business moving into Midvale."

"Alliance Chemicals' representative won't be pleased to hear that, will he?"

"I doubt it," Mr. Harcourt said dryly. "But keeping them out won't harm anyone else. There are plenty of factory jobs within twenty miles of Midvale for anyone who wants them. We don't have to let some corporation turn this town into an industrial park just to keep unemployment figures down."

Her parents went on discussing the agenda of the township meeting, but Stacy didn't join in. She had too many happy and confused thoughts buzzing in her brain to care about anyone else's conversation. Her mind kept returning to Cooper's Garage, while scenes from that afternoon's encounter kept flickering in her mind's eye, like scenes from one of the old silent movies that were sometimes telecast on Saturday afternoons.

After her parents left, Stacy hurried upstairs to the converted nursery to tackle her algebra homework. A big weekend was coming up, and the last thing she needed was unfinished schoolwork weighing her down. But concentrating was difficult.

Before she could forget, she jotted down a quick note to herself to pick up her blue wool slacks at the dry cleaner's the next day so she could wear them with her matching puff-sleeved angora sweater to Joanie Gregson's party.

She had a moment's panic when she thought about what she would have done if Nick had wanted to go out Friday instead of Saturday. It would have been unthinkable to arrive at Joanie's with him as her date. A sinking sensation filled the pit of her stomach as she imagined a sly sneer spreading over Valerie Masters's sharp features. Valerie managed to get enough mileage out of Stacy's best friend being a techie. But if her boyfriend was one as well—

Snap out of it, Stacy, she scolded herself. It was just one date, it wasn't for Friday night, and nobody at Midvale would ever have to know. Sure, it meant taking a small risk, but the image of Nick's muscles straining against the fabric of his work clothes floated in front of her eyes, and she found herself smiling.

It was a risk she was more than willing to take.

Stacy shifted in her chair and picked up her pencil, refocusing on the algebraic equations before her. This time she didn't stop until every single problem was solved. She just hoped everything else would go as simply in her life in the next few days.

SIX

As she drove toward Joanie Gregson's house Friday night, Stacy felt almost relieved Tess hadn't been invited. She thought it was cowardly of Joanie to let Valerie Masters intimidate her into snubbing Tess, although this wasn't especially surprising, since Joanie didn't seem to have a thought that wasn't something she was parroting from Valerie or their other bosom buddy, Tif Rafferty. Still, Stacy felt more than a little uncomfortable around Tess lately—since Nick had asked her out. And she kept postponing telling Tess she had a date with him for the following night.

She wouldn't have felt so guilty if Tess hadn't acted so concerned about Stacy's uncharacteristic silences. Just that day at lunchtime, Stacy had caught Tess looking at her quizzically. She had looked away, reluctant to look her friend in the eye. And of course Tess, good old sweet Tess, had said just the thing to make her feel even slimier than she already did.

"You're not still worried that you'll be a wallflower now that Rich is out of the picture, are you?" Tess had asked gently. "Just wait, Stacy, plenty of guys are going to jump at the chance to ask you out. I'll bet they'll be all over you at the party tonight." She chuckled. "I almost wish I were going, just to see Vicious Val turn pea green with envy!"

"Look over there." Glad to get the conversation away from herself, Stacy had motioned toward the far end of the room, where Valerie and Dex Grantham had their well-groomed heads together. "Looks like Valerie's going to be too busy trying to snag Dex to worry about the competition."

"They make a nice couple, don't they?" Gina had sounded wistful. "They're both so good-looking."

"Yeah, and so modest," Stacy had joked. "Right now they're probably busy telling each other how wonderful they are."

"Masters may get what she deserves, playing around with Dex," Tess had said hopefully. "Everybody knows his idea of a lasting relationship is one date. And speaking of relationships"—she turned to Stacy—"are you and Rich not speaking these days at all?"

Stacy had shrugged. "We say hi to each other in civics class, if you call that talking. I think he's got his eye on Kathy."

"Kathy Phillips?" Gina's eyes had widened. "How could he be so low? It's not right to break up with one cheerleader and immediately go after another one."

"I broke up with him, remember?" Stacy had said pointedly. It had taken an effort to hide her irritation as she added, "As far as I'm concerned, Rich has a right to go out with anyone he pleases."

"It could be awkward, though, if he starts seeing Kathy," Tess had said.

"I guess it always gets complicated when friends are involved with the same person," Stacy had said, thinking more of herself and Nick than of Rich and anybody. "Or even interested in the same person. But that's life, isn't it?"

That's life, all right, she thought, as she turned into Joanie's street, where cars were already lined up at the curb, *but that's no excuse not to have told Tess when I'd had the perfect chance.* Still, Gina was there at the time, and that was the sort of personal conversation two girls should have without an audience. *Tomorrow,* she promised herself. As soon as the game was over, she'd tell Tess her plans for the evening.

Joanie's party was no better and no worse than Stacy had expected. For the most part, she enjoyed herself, and as soon as she walked in, she realized how foolish she had been to worry about arriving dateless. "Hey, look, everybody! Stacy's here!" Joanie chirped, as if she feared somebody might miss the presence of the cheer-leading captain at her house, and within seconds Stacy was surrounded by a circle of her classmates.

As soon as she spotted Gina standing by herself in front of the stereo cabinet examining Joanie's album collection, she slipped away from the group and walked over to talk with the other cheerleader.

"Has Rich shown up yet?" she asked.

"I don't think he's coming. I heard somebody saying the Stinsons had all driven into Chicago to see a play for Mr. Stinson's birthday. Were you trying to find him or avoid him?"

"Neither, really," Stacy answered. "I was just curious." That was the truth, but she was glad to see Kathy Phillips come in with Pete Moran, a junior she'd been seeing off and on since last spring. "How come you're hiding over here by yourself?"

Gina made a face. "I'm afraid if I start having a good time, I won't want to leave. My folks went to a dinner party, but they're picking me up at ten o'clock. Can you believe it?"

"Just remember, Cinderella's story had a happy ending," Stacy teased, trying to bring a smile to Gina's fallen face.

"I think Prince Charming's busy tonight, anyway." Gina laughed, directing Stacy's attention across the room to where Dex Grantham appeared to be charming Joanie's younger sister and two other sophomore girls.

"Yeah, he sure knows how to pick 'em,"

Stacy said, glad to see a smile on Gina's lips. "Of course, Dex would flirt with anyone."

"I guess so," Gina agreed—a little jealously, Stacy thought. Maybe Gina wished flirting came easier for her. *Sometime*, Stacy told herself, *I'll have to give her some lessons.*

She didn't have a chance that evening, though. Jeremy Edwards, a transfer senior from Vermont who was in her English class, came over and asked her to dance. For the next hour or so, she stayed in the center of the floor with one boy after another, forgetting about Gina, as she was pulled into the heavy beat of the music.

Stacy was dancing with Zack Wenner when she noticed that Dave Prentice was missing. Valerie might have insisted Joanie blackball Tess, but a football player like Dave would be invited to every party. "How come Dave didn't come?" Stacy shouted to Zack over the loud music blaring from the rec-room stereo. "Do you know?"

"He told me he was going over to Tess's house," Zack shouted back. "Something about helping her study for next week's French quiz."

"But Dave's not taking French, is he? I thought he was in Mrs. Linza's Spanish class."

"Yeah, well, he says you don't have to know a language just to hold a book and quiz somebody on it." Zack let out a crude guffaw. "Maybe *studying* is a word for something else."

"Fat chance with Mr. and Mrs. Belding on the scene!" Stacy made a face. Really! Didn't some of these guys think about anything else but making out?

She glanced over at the couch against one wall, where plain, plump Mary Bowes, Zack's girlfriend, sat stiffly, a cast on one leg and a not-very-believable smile on her lips. Stacy wondered if Mary really thought she was fooling anyone, trying to appear unconcerned while her narrowed eyes never left Stacy and Zack.

As if she'd be interested in a muscle-bound hulk like Zack, whose idea of being smooth was slapping a girl on the fanny! Still, she took pity on Mary, who probably would have loved to be out there dancing herself. She pulled away as Zack reached to take her in his arms for a slow number. "I need something to drink—and I'll bet Mary could use a little company."

Without waiting for him to answer, she slipped away and crossed to the bar, which was piled high with cold cuts and soft drinks.

Valerie was perched atop one of the bar stools, the better to show off her tan suede skirt and vest. She broke off from flirting with Dex Grantham long enough to smile at Stacy, a smile that didn't reach her cold blue eyes.

"Nice sweater, Stacy," she purred. "I almost wore my angora tonight, but of course, it sheds so badly on suede." She stretched with catlike grace, a calculated movement that caused her creamy satin shirt to shimmer under the track lighting.

What a cat Valerie is, Stacy thought as she

poured herself a drink, *always ready to bare her claws*. Smiling sweetly, she thanked the other girl for the compliment, then looked bleakly around the room. "I didn't see Dave Prentice," she said, feigning puzzlement. "Don't tell me Joanie didn't invite him."

That remark wiped away Valerie's pleasant expression. "Don't ask me," she snapped. "After all, it's not *my* party."

"You know Val's only in charge of which *girls* don't get invited," Dex quipped, smirking. As Valerie wheeled around, ready to lash out at him, he stroked her satiny shoulder. "Come on, Val, you know how I like to tease you." Stacy nearly choked on her cola as she turned away.

Because the first game of the season was being played the next day, the party broke up just after midnight. Stacy didn't mind. As much as she liked most of the kids at Joanie's and enjoyed hanging out with them, tonight she had found that the shallowness of Valerie and her friends stood out more sharply than usual. She'd been downright irritated by some of their stupid comments.

Sometimes those kids act like spoiled brats, she thought wearily as she pulled closed her car door and headed home. If people like Valerie and Dex lost their looks and couldn't afford to buy great clothes and be up on all the latest trends, their popularity would evaporate overnight. Nick Cooper probably didn't think twice about who'd designed his shirts, and if anybody ever gave him a jersey with a little animal sewed on the chest, he'd probably cut it off. Would Nick have sympathized with Valerie because angora shed on suede? Some of the Midvale kids had no idea what the real world was like.

As if the elements knew football season started that day, Saturday marked the first real change in the weather, as fall made its presence felt. Stacy was so full of energy when she popped out of bed at ten-thirty, she decided to jog before brunch.

Running had been last year's craze at school, and all of Stacy's friends had acquired stylish running wardrobes. One section of Stacy's closet was filled with pastel warm-up suits and sweat suits in vivid colors. *But I really work out in them*, she told herself proudly as she flicked through the hangers, finally deciding on rose-colored sweatpants with a contrasting pale mauve sweatshirt. *Not like Valerie and Joanie and Tif.* Valerie's clique had lost interest in fitness early on and now wore their running gear to *look* athletic rather than to actually do anything about it.

Stacy didn't get to run nearly as often as she'd have liked—she was too busy to find the time. Now, as she brushed blush across her cheekbones and applied mauve lip gloss, she decided she'd have to arrange her schedule to fit more jogging in. She always felt so much better for having worked out.

She'd try to do two miles or so, she decided as she left the house. Maybe she could soon work up to four or five miles, or even to running in the Easter Bunny Hop-A-Thon in the spring. With enthusiasm, she started on her way, listening with satisfaction to the *slap-slap* of her running shoes as she headed toward the corner.

Within fifteen minutes, she was back, pouring herself a big bowl of cornflakes in the kitchen. It would be silly to begin a major running regimen before the season's first game, she had decided as the first stitch had sneaked into her side midway around the block. Fitness wouldn't help her if she twisted her ankle and got sidelined from cheering for the rest of the season.

She had the house all to herself: Emma was spending the whole weekend with her son's family on the other side of town, and Stacy's parents had driven up to Michigan in the wee hours of the morning to spend the day with Sarah.

Stacy would have loved to have gone with them, but with cheering duties every weekend, there was no chance of her making any full-day trips. She missed Sarah more than she'd ever thought she would in the days when her sister was monopolizing the bathroom mirror. At least she knew she would be seeing her sometime soon, since Sarah was certain to come home for their mother's birthday in November.

The phone rang as Stacy was making herself

a grilled cheese and tomato on rye later that afternoon. It was Tess, asking if Stacy could pick her up on the way to the high school later on. "It's no problem for me, but how come you aren't taking your own car?" she asked, thinking how complicated everything would be if Tess expected her to drive the two of them to Nicola's after the game.

She relaxed as Tess said, "Since it's a home game and I'll be going out with Dave afterward, it seems silly to take my car, too, so I thought I'd just hitch a ride with you. That way you can fill me in on all the gory details of Valerie's party, too."

"Will do," Stacy promised. "Listen, my grilled cheese is going to be charcoal if I don't flip it right now!"

She added chips and pickle slices to her plate, then poured herself a big glass of milk and sat down at the kitchen table for a leisurely meal. As she rinsed off the dishes and put them in the dishwasher for Emma, she decided it was a good thing she'd eaten a late lunch. Who knew what Nick Cooper's idea of a date would be? Chances were it wouldn't include anything resembling a meal, so she might have to wait and grab a quick makeshift supper when she got home. As it was, she'd have two hours to herself now, plenty of time to take a leisurely bubble bath, wash and dry her hair, and polish her nails. It was important for a cheerleader to look her best at every game, and she loved having time on her hands with nothing to do but pamper herself.

Usually, she just wore her uniform and kept it on after the game. But today, she'd take a change of clothes along so she could switch outfits in the girls' locker room afterward. Nick might feel self-conscious being seen with a girl wearing Midvale's distinctive blue-and-gold cheering outfit. *But just what*, Stacy wondered as she riffled through the racks in her closet, *is the right thing to wear for a date with a mechanic?*

She finally settled on jeans, boots, and a rust-colored bulky-knit turtleneck that highlighted the golden streaks in her hair. She caught herself humming merrily under her breath as she ran the bathwater, watching the pink porcelain bathtub turn into a lagoon of fragrant foam. She hadn't realized just how much she looked forward to cheering at the first game of the season.

After her bath, Stacy folded her change of clothes and tucked them into her duffel bag with the necessities she and most of the other squad members took to each game: hairbrush, styling mousse, makeup, a candy bar in case she was starving by half time, extra tights.

Tess came running out the front door the instant Stacy tooted her horn. "I can't believe today's really here, can you?" Tess asked. Without waiting for an answer, she went on, "The first game of the season! And this year I'll be rooting for Dave! What about my hair? Does it look all right like this? I thought if I pulled it back a little, it wouldn't flop all over my face so much when I cheer." She reached up and fidgeted with one of the silver barrettes that pulled her curly locks away from her cheeks on each side.

When Stacy nodded, Tess said, "Okay, it's your turn to talk. How was the party last night?"

"The usual," Stacy answered. "Valerie striking poses all over the place, Joanie twittering around, good music, and tons of food. You didn't miss much—except for the look on Val's face when I asked why Dave wasn't there. Pure poison!"

"That witch!" Tess giggled. "Dave told me he had a much better time with me than he would have had at Joanie's."

"Oh?" Stacey asked innocently. "I didn't realize he liked studying all that much."

"I guess it depends on who he studies with." Tess's voice vibrated with pleasure. "Oh, Stacy, you were right! How could I have even considered looking at another boy? Do you know what he did last night?" she asked. "He showed up with a single white rose for me, because I'd once said they were my favorite. And you know why? Because it was exactly one month since our first date. Now, isn't that the most romantic thing you've ever heard?"

"That's great, Tess!" Stacy enthused, relief mixing with genuine happiness for her friend's obvious bliss. After all, if Tess really was getting serious about Dave, it proved she was never all that interested in Nick Cooper in the first place. "I told you he was special."

"He makes me feel special." Tess laughed again, sounding so crazily happy that Stacy was almost jealous.

But as she turned into the high-school parking lot, Stacy was flooded with relief. It was as if a giant weight had been magically lifted from her shoulders. *Now,* she thought, *I won't have to tell Tess about Nick at all*. It certainly wasn't important any longer. She'd stepped in just in time and kept her best friend from making a big mistake. There was no reason to let Tess know how Stacy had gone out of her way to help her.

SEVEN

"We're the Midvale Mustangs,
Gold and blue.
We're going to beat Brownville
Before we're through.

"C'mon, Mustangs,
Get that ball.
Make those mighty
Bearcats crawl!"

Bringing her megaphone to her mouth, Stacy ran onto the field in front of the home-team bleachers, leading the cheer that would open the fourth quarter. The floodlights had been lit against the gathering dusk, and as she dropped the megaphone to execute a perfectly arched back jump, she caught sight of her hair billowing out to one side, glistening like spun gold.

Stacy loved cheering. She felt more alive down on the field than she did anywhere else.

And it wasn't just because she was the center of attention. Part of her satisfaction came from knowing she was doing her part to help Midvale win, stirring up the team spirit and encouraging the crowd to go all out in cheering their players to glory.

Not that the Mustangs need a lot of help in this game, she thought, watching them go for a first down and come up barely a yard short. Admiring the fresh pale mauve polish on her nails as she once again brought her hands to her mouth, she called out to the other girls in the squad, "Second down cheer! Let's go!"

The score was twenty-one to six, and everyone was pretty sure the Mustangs were going to win. But that was when cheering was important, in Stacy's opinion. She had reminded her fellow cheerleaders of just that during half time, while the Brownville band performed. "It's easy to get the crowd to yell its lungs out when we're behind. We've got to remember it's important to keep the cheering loud and clear when we're ahead, too. It's never too late for the other side to come from behind and mow our guys down, remember. And they've got the second half to do it in. So let's keep our spirit high, girls!"

As captain, she certainly couldn't complain about the day's cheering. The new cheer Gina had created was a winner, and all the juniors had worked extra hard to perfect it. Tess had practically bruised her palms whooping and clapping when Dave made a spectacular dash to score the second touchdown of the game, and even though it was against official squad rules, Stacy hadn't had the heart to ask her friend to remove the white rose pinned to her top.

After Stacy's halftime pep talk, all six cheerleaders had dashed to the girls' locker room to repair their hair and makeup. They'd all laughed as Tess said with regret, "It breaks my heart to miss Valerie out there twirling away." At that moment, Stacy felt so close to the other girls on the squad, it was almost as if they were all one person. That was the best part of cheering, maybe, even better than the attention and the glory. It was a sort of sisterhood, really, and the six who'd been chosen shared a special bond unlike any other.

"I wonder if Mom and Dad made it here," Tess had remarked thoughtfully as she smudged smoky blue eye pencil beneath her lower lids, then stepped back to study herself in the mirror. "Mom had to work till four today, but they figured they could get here for the second half."

"My folks wouldn't miss a game," Sherri Callahan had said as she gingerly worked a dollop of mousse through her deep auburn curls. "Of course, they'd be at every game even if I wasn't cheering," she'd added, and everyone nodded. Sherri's brother Dennis was one of those seniors the others teased about being an "activities major." Besides being editor of the *Sentinel*, he was president of the chess and science clubs, cocaptain of the track team, and drum major.

"My folks couldn't come this week," Stacy had chimed in, mumbling a little as she dabbed clear gloss over her lipstick. "They promised my sister weeks ago they'd drive up to school to spend the day. It's her sorority's open house. Did your mom and dad come?" she'd asked Gina.

As soon as she'd seen the other girl shake her head in the mirror, Stacy had wondered why she'd been dumb enough to ask. Gina's folks had never come to a single extracurricular event at the school that she knew of—which was surprising, since they seemed determined to keep an eagle eye on their daughter. "I think they were taking Dino to the movies, to see that new *Star Wars* rip-off." She had laughed. "I think he was taking them, actually. Can you imagine anyone wanting to see an outer space adventure story more than their nine-year-old son?"

"You mean your folks admit they like that stuff?" Patricia had asked in amazement.

"Dad's an engineering professor and Mama's a computer operator at Adler Aeronautics, remember? They insist they only see these things for professional reasons." She had rolled her eyes.

"Football's what fall's all about around my house," Kathy Phillips had said. "I guess Mom learned about the plays and the lingo just so she could have conversations with somebody between August and New Year's! What about your folks, Pixie? . . . Oh, sorry, I meant Patricia."

Patricia's usually elfin features had twisted into a sneer of disdain. "Oh, let's see, I think Dad had a date with this stewardess he's seeing who can't be much older than I am. They were going horseback riding, so he should manage to make a total fool of himself. Mom had her 'Women in Transition' lunch meeting, then she was going to go get a perm and a facial. I suppose she figures if Dad's going to date somebody young enough to be his daughter, she's not going to be caught dead looking like an old bag."

Everyone had been silent, and Stacy could tell by Kathy's pained look that she was scolding herself for forgetting about Patricia's parents' divorce. The Petersens had split up during the summer, and Patricia had confessed she'd felt like a Ping-Pong ball ever since, spending half the time at home in the sprawling split-level that had once been home to the whole family and the rest of the time at what her father called his "bachelor pad," a posh apartment on Chicago's Near North Side.

"C'mon, snap out of it," Patricia had said at last with a harsh laugh. "It's not as if anybody died. I mean, they're having the time of their lives, him with his Jacuzzi and rooftop health club, and her with all those other divorced women she goes out with. And between the two of them trying to win me over, I'm getting twice the allowance and more clothes than I had before, so I guess I can't complain. And I don't have to put a pillow over my head to drown out their yelling at each other anymore."

"I'll bet that's the best part of all," Tess had said, sounding so strange that Stacy had looked up sharply. Were the Beldings really arguing all that much? Then Tess had shaken out her curls and said in her normally bubbly way, "Hey, this is no way to get ourselves psyched up for the second half! Come on," she'd urged, linking her arm through Stacy's, "let's sing 'On, Mighty Mustangs' and go back out there looking like winners!"

Now Stacy watched proudly as the Mustangs racked up one score after another, feeling only a tiny pang when she had to lead a "Let's hear it for Stinson" cheer. Watching Rich in all his glory on the field, looking more broad shouldered and agile than ever in the deep blue jersey widened by bulky shoulder pads, wasn't as irritating as she'd been afraid it might be. Sure, he'd be one of the players—along with Dave and Zack—who'd be slapped on the back and congratulated at the pizza parlor after the game. But Stacy no longer had to worry about sharing the spotlight with him tonight—she'd be with Nick Cooper, whose movie-idol looks put even Rich's clean-cut attractiveness to shame.

The Mustangs won a lopsided victory, and all the cheerleaders basked in the shared glory as they led a rousing cheer for the home team. *Triumph is contagious*, Stacy thought as she jogged along with the others toward the locker room. During the last quarter, she'd been aware that all the girls were jumping higher and more energetically than at practice or earlier in the game. Gina's jumps were always perfect, since she had a dancer's grace and a gymnast's power, but today Stacy had noticed that Tess's split kicks had really come a long way, with even more extension than Gina's. *I'll have to remember to suggest spotlighting Tess in an upcoming cheer*, she thought, making a mental note to bring it up at practice soon.

"How come you're changing?" Tess asked when Stacy headed straight for her locker and pulled out the clothes she'd stashed there. "I meant to ask you that before. There's no new rule about not wearing our uniforms after the games, is there?"

"Uh-uh." Stacy's voice was muffled as she pulled her sweater over her head. "We can wear them as long as we want any day there's a game."

"You didn't answer my first question," Tess reminded her as they fought for space at the makeup mirror.

"Oh, well—" Stacy hesitated. Should she tell the truth, after all? Then her eyes lit on the rose that Tess was wearing, and she thought, *Why risk stirring up trouble when Tess is so happy?*

"My folks said they'd be back early, so we'll probably go out to dinner," she answered.

"But they know you always hang out with us after a game!" Tess protested.

"To be perfectly honest," Stacy went on, lowering her voice, "I'd just as soon not be around while everybody's raving about Rich's game. I just wouldn't feel right."

"Of course." Tess nodded understandingly. "I don't suppose I'd want to watch everybody fawning all over Dave if I wasn't seeing him anymore."

Glad to get away from the subject of her own plans before she was led into any more white lies, Stacy grinned as she finished dabbing on lip gloss with her little finger. "As it is, you'll be right there by his side. I'm so glad it's working out between the two of—"

"Shh!" Tess jabbed her in the ribs, and Stacy could see Valerie approaching them, her reflection edging closer to theirs in the mirror.

"Yeah, it sure was a great game," she said quickly, as if that was all she and Tess had been discussing. No use giving Valerie any fuel she might use to burn down Tess's self-confidence. "I'd better run," she said as she moved away, adding, "but maybe I'll catch up with you later."

She was still wondering why she'd said that as she pulled her car into the lot at Cooper's Garage, carefully steering it around toward the far side where it would be hidden from the highway by a tow truck and a couple of vans.

The last thing she wanted to do tonight was run into anyone from Midvale. If Nick suggested going anyplace local, she'd have to think of some way to convince him to change his mind without making it seem as if she didn't want to be seen as his date.

Nick was alone in the cluttered small office when she walked in, and a look of such clear-cut relief spread over his rugged features at the sight of her that Stacy suspected he'd been worried she wouldn't show up. She felt a little shiver as she smiled and said hi. What girl wouldn't like knowing she had a guy like Nick waiting eagerly for her?

"You look like Midvale must have won the game," he said, getting to his feet, but Stacy could tell it didn't matter much to Nick which school had emerged victorious. "My uncle's already split and I locked up the garage bays, so I've just got to close up and we can go."

His eyes flicked briefly toward her as he tugged at the top drawer of the old steel desk and removed a heavy brass ring of keys. "Nice outfit," he murmured gruffly. "You look nice."

"Thanks." She leaned against the door as she watched him checking the locks on the file cabinets, glad he'd taken his eyes off her so he couldn't see the flush rising in her cheeks. *Why am I suddenly feeling so tongue-tied and silly,* she asked herself, furious with the shyness that was sweeping over her. *Why, he's hardly said anything!*

Dex Grantham would have gone on and on about how gorgeous she was, what a sexy sweater she had on. And she probably wouldn't have batted an eye.

But here she was, feeling heat rise from her toes to the tips of her ears, and all because Nick Cooper had thrown her a clumsy compliment, even having to use "nice" twice, since he couldn't come up with a better word.

She noticed his own clothes as he came around to her side of the desk. It was what she thought of as the typical techie uniform: black chinos, boots, flannel shirt checkered in red and black. *Of course, Nick can wear clothes like that and look incredibly attractive,* she told herself, as he grabbed a beat-up black leather bomber jacket from the coat rack. On Nick, they had—well, character.

As he hit the switch to douse the lights and held the door open for her, a glimmer from the single bulb over the door seeped inside, spotlighting the hollows beneath his high cheekbones, the sharp square line of his jaw. Then they were outside, and he was turning to lock the door behind him.

"Jimmy, this guy I know from the speedway, is having a party tonight. I thought we could stop by there." He looked at her uncertainly.

"Great!" She didn't have to fake her enthusiasm—she was just glad they'd be going someplace where kids from Midvale wouldn't see them.

"Here we are," Nick said, pride ringing in his voice. Stacy stopped dead, staring at a shiny black Trans Am, raised high in the back by its oversized rear wheels. "This is what I race in."

"Nice," she murmured, unable to find another word to describe the beast Nick obviously took pride in.

"She's a real beauty, isn't she?" he asked, unlocking the door on the passenger side and holding it open for her.

"I've never seen anything quite like it," Stacy admitted truthfully as she slid into the front seat, glad he was already walking around to the other side and couldn't see her eyes widen in horror as she saw the stenciled red enamel flames that swept up across the hood.

All it needs is a pair of foam dice hanging from the rear-view mirror, she thought. As Nick got in and switched on the ignition, Stacy felt one part of her float outside and look down on the scene from above. Stacy Harcourt sitting in some souped-up hunk of metal next to a guy in a black leather jacket? Who'd ever have believed it? It was all she could do not to laugh!

Then Nick was turning to her, the tip of one index finger tracing a light, lazy line down her cheek and beneath her jaw. "I'm glad you could make it tonight, Stacy," he said softly. "I really am."

Then both his hands were on the wheel and the car was heading onto the highway with a loud rumble of exhaust.

And Stacy didn't feel a bit like laughing anymore. At that moment, there was no place else she'd rather have been.

EIGHT

At Joanie Gregson's party the night before, Stacy had walked into the room and immediately commanded the attention of every boy and girl. At Jimmy Burdett's, she felt more out of place than she could remember since she'd been a little girl on the first day of kindergarten.

Jimmy Burdett didn't even live in a house with his parents. His place was a house trailer on the edge of a woods down a dirt road. When Nick had turned left off the two-lane blacktop that cut through miles of grain fields, Stacy noticed a sign pointing in the opposite direction from Jimmy's that said Watson's Grove.

The crowd was older, for the most part, and the few kids Stacy learned were her own age all looked about ten years older. Most of the guys had mustaches or beards, while the girls wore more makeup than Stacy, making her feel both childish and dowdy.

The first thing Stacy noticed when she and Nick pushed their way into the tiny kitchen of the cramped trailer was the bar set up on the Formica kitchen counter, an array of beer cans and liquor bottles. Stacy definitely wasn't allowed at parties where alcohol was served. But how could she tell Nick she'd have to leave without sounding like a baby?

He saved her from her dilemma. "Let's get a couple of sodas and try to find a space where it's less crowded," he suggested, elbowing his way to the counter. As long as neither she nor her date drank anything but soft drinks, Stacy decided, it was the same as a regular party. She could just forget she saw those beer cans and bottles.

"I didn't know there'd be such a mob!" Nick shouted over the heavily amplified Bob Seger music as he steered Stacy through a narrow, short hallway. "Jimmy won a race yesterday, so I guess he's celebrating."

Stacy just nodded. She didn't know quite what to say or how to act. When Nick introduced her to a girl with teased blond hair and heavily black-rimmed eyes a few minutes later, saying, "Stacy, this is Margie, Jimmy's girl," she could only nod and try to smile and look friendly and relaxed.

Luckily, Margie didn't seem as tough as she looked. She smiled warmly, an expression that transformed her into a teenaged girl. "Sorry it's so loud," she apologized, almost yelling to make herself heard over the music. "Jimmy says the best thing about living so far out is being able to play the stereo as loud as he wants. My pop flips out if I put a record on loud enough to be able to hear the lyrics, so I kind of like it."

Stacy simply nodded again, too transfixed by the sight of the triple gold studs in Margie's ears to think of something to say. She was afraid if she opened her mouth, Margie would wonder why Nick wanted to go out with some silly high-school girl. She didn't quite know why she felt that way—after all, wasn't Nick in high school himself? She only knew how glad she was that she hadn't shown up in her cheerleading jumper. At least in her jeans and sweater, she didn't stick out like a sore thumb.

She glanced toward Nick, wishing he'd pick up the conversation and rescue her, but he was no help. He was bellowing over the loud music, having an animated discussion about cars with a T-shirted guy who must have been Jimmy.

Stacy was struggling to find something to say to Margie when the other girl asked, "You still in school?"

"I'm a senior at Midvale," Stacy shouted back, wishing she could find something intelligent to say and stop nodding so much; she felt like one of those fuzzy dogs whose heads bobbled in the back windows of old jalopies.

"I would have been a senior at Carson this year, but I dropped out last spring," Margie confided. "I kind of miss school, I guess."

"Do you think you'll go back?" Stacy asked, curious to learn more about this girl now that she knew they were the same age. Margie was so different!

"Aw, I doubt it. See, with six brothers and sisters at home, I never got much time to study and I always had to work after school to help out, anyhow. So I finally thought, why not work full time? At least this way I can pay Pop my room and board."

"Where do you work?" Stacy asked, wondering how she'd feel if her parents expected her to come up with money for room and board and admiring Margie for being so matter-of-fact about the whole thing.

"Right now I'm at the donut shop over on Route Eighty-three," Margie answered. "But I'm on the waiting list at a couple of factories over in Brownville. To do piecework, you know. It pays a lot more. Of course, if this Alliance Chemicals company opens in Midvale, I'll try to get in there."

Stacy nodded again before she could stop herself, wishing she knew what piecework was so she could say something but not willing to admit her ignorance. And she wasn't going to touch the subject of Alliance Chemicals, not when her own father was leading the campaign to keep their factory out of Midvale.

Nick turned back toward them then, introducing Stacy to Jimmy. He seemed less outgoing than his girlfriend and smiled shyly, looking like a big bashful bear. "You're looking pretty slick tonight," Nick teased Margie flirtatiously.

"Jimmy'd better try to keep an eye on the stands while he's racing, make sure all those guys aren't trying to steal his girl, hitting on you all the time."

Margie giggled. "Bright idea, Sherlock! How many races do you think Jimmy's going to win if he's not watching the track?"

They talked a little longer, and Stacy listened eagerly, wishing she could swap shoptalk with Nick with the ease Margie was displaying. It didn't bother her that most of their racing terminology and car talk—stuff about "camshafts" and "superchargers"—was over her head. It was fascinating, and she liked the idea that Nick was introducing her to his life-style.

"Hey, if you guys are hungry, there's food out in back," Margie told them. "Jimmy's brother Benny is playing chef on the barbecue grill. We've got hot dogs and burgers and all kinds of goodies."

"Hungry?" Nick asked Stacy thoughtfully.

She'd forgotten about eating since the grilled cheese sandwich earlier, but now she realized she was ravenous. "To tell the truth, I'm starving," she admitted.

"Let's go," he said, taking her hand in his and leading her through the mob of people and out the trailer door. In the front clearing, couples were starting to dance to the loud music, but out back it was quieter and the air was fragrant with the mingled odors of charcoal and meat.

"Some party, huh?" Nick asked after they'd filled two paper plates and were sitting side by side on a redwood bench back by the trees. "Old Jimmy knows how to do it right."

"It sure isn't like the usual Midvale parties I go to," Stacy said.

"How come?" Nick asked. "Do they have butlers passing those crazy little cocktail sausages on a silver plate or something?"

"Of course not, silly! They're just—oh, I don't know, more low-key, I suppose. All the same old people and everybody kind of being on best behavior and worrying what everybody else thinks of them. No one's letting everything hang out like they are here. This is definitely the loudest party I've ever been to."

"Does it bother you?" Nick sounded concerned. "I mean, you must have had more than your share of screaming and shouting at the football game."

"Oh, no," she said quickly. "This is great. I mean, everyone's having such a good time." She grinned as shouts of laughter reached them over the music. "I think it's a good idea to let your hair down and get rowdy. Everyone here seems really ready to party." She was afraid Nick had noticed her quietness and chalked it up to her not liking his friends instead of realizing how unsure of herself she suddenly felt. She added, "I've just got a bit of a headache, that's all. It's not the music," she continued. "It was just all that cheering earlier."

She hated herself for sounding so apologetic—until Nick took the plate from her and set it on top of his on the ground, looking at her sweetly.

"Poor thing . . . I should have remembered Jimmy's idea of good music means it's got to be as loud as a police siren." He put his arm around her, and she leaned against him, feeling the strength and warmth of his hand even through her bulky sweater. "Tell you what. I'll sneak in and grab a couple more cans of pop, and we'll get out of here and find some peace and quiet."

She felt more like herself again when they were back in Nick's car, and she was so relieved to get away from the party where she'd been so out of place that the gleaming, streamlined Trans Am no longer looked like a monstrosity. Instead, it felt familiar and cozy.

"You said you'd never been to the Grove, right?" Nick asked as he pulled out onto the dirt track leading away from Jimmy's. "We'll take a ride over there."

"Is that going to be quiet with all those stock cars zooming around?"

"You don't have to worry about that," Nick assured her. "There are no races tonight. Just Friday nights and Saturday afternoons. This time of night, we'll have the place to ourselves."

Stacy sank back against the seat, sipping her

soft drink straight from the can, content to listen to the music wafting from the car's speakers. She felt much better being alone with Nick than she had at the party.

Now that Jimmy's trailer was miles away, she felt a little foolish at not having made more of an effort to join in the fun. She hadn't been lying when she'd assured Nick that she thought it was a great party. At least she hadn't been smothered by that same-old-thing-again feeling she remembered from Joanie Gregson's. Maybe Jimmy and Margie weren't the sort of people she felt at ease with yet, but at least they weren't spoiled and shallow like Valerie's crowd. At least they were *real*.

The car turned off one dirt road onto another. "Here's the picnic area and the campgrounds," Nick was saying. "Sometimes, when there's a championship race or a semifinals on, you'll find as many as two hundred campers and vans and trailers here. They come from all over to drive at the Grove. See, up here's the track."

Ahead of them she could see acres of chainlink fencing, and behind the fence, the racetrack itself, with a semicircle of high bleachers at its edge. A few security lights were shining down, but the place was deserted. It looked ghostly but not dangerous.

Nick pulled to a stop at the fence and switched off the engine, turning the ignition key so the tape would keep playing. He leaned back and slid down in the seat slightly, sighing. "I love this place. It doesn't look like much now, but, boy, wait until you see it when there's racing going on. It comes alive then! See, over there are the pits . . ."

As Nick explained the racetrack, Stacy only half-listened. What he was saying now wasn't as interesting as what he'd already said. "Wait until you see it when there's racing going on," he'd said. Her pulse quickened as the words echoed in her ears.

Hadn't she told herself this would be her only date with Nick, that once would be enough?

But as his arm slipped around her shoulders and pulled her closer to him, she knew once wouldn't be enough. Just being next to Nick made her tingle, and when his lips met hers, it was as if an electric current passed between the two of them. Suddenly everything was right.

She had never felt this way with Rich. The shivery warmth that went straight to her heart, the feeling that she was melting in Nick's arms— it was what she had dreamed of.

It wasn't just that Nick's kisses were gentler and more expert than Rich's had been, though that was undeniably true. Rich had kissed just like every other boy she'd kissed before now. But Nick's technique was special. When his lips weren't on hers, they were brushing her neck or her face or her hair.

She'd never responded to any boy before as

she did to Nick, her lips as hungry as his as she pressed closer to him in a way that would have seemed too eager with Rich. With Nick, it was heaven.

When she finally pulled away from him fifteen minutes or so later, whispering, "I can't, Nick . . . I've got to go home now," the regret trembling in her voice was genuine. In his arms, she'd felt truly alive. But it was their first date, and she couldn't risk his getting the wrong idea about her. She had no idea what sort of girls he was used to.

"I could stay here with you for hours, Stacy." His voice was hoarse, almost harsh, but the fingers entwined in hers were gentle.

"I know," she agreed, "but it's late. And I've still got to drive home from the garage."

"Yeah, I guess you're right." Reluctantly, he let her go, taking a deep breath as he straightened his shoulders and started the car. "We'll have to come for a race or two some night," he said in a more even tone as they drove off. "I'll bet you've never seen anything like this track when it's really jumping."

"Oh, I don't know," she teased lightly. "I liked it all right with nobody else around."

He took one hand off the wheel to reach down and pat her knee, which warmed to his touch through the heavy denim of her jeans. "I liked it a lot myself."

Neither of them spoke again until they were

in the lot at Cooper's. *It's as if there's no need for words*, Stacy thought contentedly. Hadn't their kisses said it all?

One last kiss, then Nick told her, "If I don't get a chance to talk to you around school, I'll call you at home at night. Okay?"

"Okay," she agreed, adding, "that number's my own phone, so you can call any time."

"You've got a private phone, huh?" He whistled. "Pretty fancy."

"Oh, not really," she said quickly, afraid she'd said something that might put him off. "It's just that my parents say they like to get phone calls, too, and they were afraid I'd have the line tied up so nobody could get through."

"I'll talk to you soon," he promised.

He waited there while she walked to her car, started the motor, and pulled away. Then he followed her out of the lot. Stacy liked that. It made her feel special and protected.

She drove home half in a daze, having to will herself to pay attention to the sparse late-night traffic and concentrate on the road. She could still feel Nick's lips on hers, still taste them, and the leathery scent of his jacket continued to cling to her.

She remembered the last time she'd been kissed—by Rich—and how impossible it had been to explain why his kisses weren't enough. She'd known then she wanted something more.

And now she knew she'd found it. With

Nick Cooper, she'd experienced the lightheaded joy she knew a boy should cause. How could she have imagined one date would have been enough?

NINE

Monday morning, Stacy found herself looking this way and that every time she walked down a corridor or up a staircase from one class to another, hoping she'd run into Nick, even though she knew he probably took most of his classes in the vo-tech workshops, which were in the separate one-story wing adjoining the main three-story brick school building.

She practically ran into him on the way to lunch, when she wasn't even scouring the halls in the hope of sighting him. "Hey!" he said with a grin, the dimple in his cheek deepening and his eyes lighting up with pleasure in that way that turned Stacy's knees to watery Jell-O. "Aren't you the busy cheerleader rushing all over the place!"

"Hi, Nick. I'm just going to lunch, no place special. Guess I should watch where I'm going, huh?" Her voice sounded like another person's to her ears, all breathy and quivering and uncertain. "That's a nice sweater you've got on."

"Thanks." He looked sweet and shy, his eyes aimed at the scuffed brown linoleum on the floor, his chestnut hair shimmering under the glaring fluorescent lights. "My sister gave it to me last Christmas. She said I wore too much black and needed something bright. Guess she couldn't find anything much brighter than this."

"I've always liked red," Stacy told him. "Especially on men. Anyhow, your sister's got good taste. And you look nice in it."

He looked up then, flushing nearly enough to make him look color coordinated. "You'll have to meet Cora sometime. I'll bet the two of you would hit it off. . . . Hey, isn't this week's game on Friday night? I've got a day off coming. We could stop by my sister's house for lunch Saturday, then head out to the Grove and catch a couple of races. What do you think?"

"Sure, I'd love to," she answered eagerly, gazing into the warmth of Nick's brown eyes, noticing for the first time how the irises were flecked with little bits of gold like a tiger's-eye.

"Great!" Bells started clanging then, almost drowning out his next words. "Look, I've got to run. I don't have lunch till next period, and I've got to get all the way to the third floor for my next class. But I'll call you soon, okay?"

"Okay," she murmured, turning to watch the straight set of his wide shoulders and the slimness of his hips, the long strides of his legs as he walked away. She pushed through the swinging doors of the cafeteria with bells ringing in her head as loudly as the ones resounding through the corridors.

She spotted Tess and Gina sitting at their usual table, along with Janet Perry and Marsha Steiner, both seniors. She got in line, put a tuna melt, coleslaw, pudding, and a container of milk on her tray, then headed over their way.

"Hi, everybody," she said, plopping herself down in an empty seat across from Tess. "What's the matter, Gina? How come you're not eating?"

Tess gave her an odd look, but Gina answered her question in a perfectly normal voice. "Oh, I've got some things to do, so I'm not staying. I'll eat lunch in the gym. I brought it from home."

"Not a bad idea under the circumstances." Stacy wrinkled her nose. "How do they always manage to make the tuna melt cold enough for the cheese to congeal when the milk's always lukewarm? It can't be easy."

"Be glad you didn't take the beef and tomato casserole," Marsha told her—while Tess just sat there with a look that closed down her usually open features. "It tasted like dog meat and ketchup."

"Now I'm really glad I brought a sandwich," Gina said. She pushed back her chair and stood up. "I'd better run. If you want to stay after cheering practice, I'll go over that new jump routine with you, Tess."

"Would you? I sure could use some pointers," Tess said warmly. Now Stacy was sure Tess was acting strangely—and just as sure Tess's strange attitude was directed only toward her.

Janet's eyes sparkled as she leaned across the table toward Stacy. "You'll never guess what just happened," she said, her voice low but excited. "I was just telling Tess."

"Whatever it is, it must be good. You've got an expression like a Cheshire cat's."

"Dennis Callahan asked me to go out with him Saturday!"

"Dennis?" Stacy gulped so that she wouldn't choke on her mouthful of coleslaw. "But I thought Dennis was too busy with all his activities for dating. He always acts so above that sort of thing."

"I guess the poor boy's finally realized he's missing something in life," Janet said, sounding only half-kidding. "You know I'm on the *Sentinel* staff this year, right? Well, ever since school started, he's been going out of his way to kid me about one thing or another, especially my new haircut. He called it the prisoner-of-war look," she said with a chuckle, running the fingers of one hand through her short brownish-blond hair, which couldn't have been more than an inch long anywhere on her head.

"Now tell her how romantic he was when he asked you out at the *Sentinel* work session this morning," Marsha prompted her.

Janet giggled. "He told me he'd always wanted to go out with a girl whose hair was shorter than his. Anyhow, I could tell he was nervous—his hands were perspiring all over the proof sheet."

"So you've got a date with Dennis? I always thought he was pretty cute myself," Stacy said, though, truthfully, she thought Dennis Callahan was peculiar-looking and that Sherri had gotten all the looks in that family. Still, there were probably girls who wouldn't think Nick Cooper was gorgeous, difficult as it was for Stacy to imagine.

"Tess says we can go to the movies with her and Dave if we want. What do you think, Stacy? You always seem to know how to get guys to relax."

"Oh, I'd say go to the movies with Dave and Tess," Stacy agreed before sinking her teeth into her sandwich.

"Speaking of your talent for getting guys to relax," Tess said, a tinge of sarcasm coloring her normally bright voice, "I noticed you were doing okay with Nick Cooper in the hallway just a minute ago. You were both so relaxed you didn't even see me walk right by." She raised her eyebrows. "And to think that just a week ago you didn't even know who he was."

Stacy had been raising what was left of her sandwich to take another bite. She froze, her hand in midair. Now she knew what shoplifters felt like when they were caught in the act of slipping unpaid-for goods into their shopping bags. She set the sandwich back on her plate, stalling for time.

She smiled, hoping she looked calmer than she felt. "I guess I owe you a thank-you for introducing us," she said lightly. "You kept telling me what a good mechanic he was, so when my car acted up yesterday after the game"—one little white lie couldn't hurt—"I headed for Cooper's and, um, I ended up going to this party with Nick. He just asked me out for this weekend, so . . ." She paused, then went on with a slightly nervous giggle, "So I guess I'm not a wallflower anymore."

A silence fell over the table, and Stacy didn't dare look at Tess. It was broken only when Janet and Marsha asked in unison, "Who's Nick Cooper?"

"Oh, you two wouldn't know him," Tess answered quite matter-of-factly. "He's in vo-tech." She laughed.

Stacy stared at her friend in surprise—and with more than a little relief. *Why, Tess doesn't sound the least bit annoyed. Of course, there's no reason she should be, since she has a boyfriend of her own. Still . . .* It was only when her friend spoke again that Stacy realized what was wrong. Tess sounded genuinely *amused.*

"I can't believe it, Stacy!" she exclaimed. "Can you two believe it?" she asked Janet and Marsha. "I mean, Stacy Harcourt going out with a techie!"

"C'mon, Tess, lay off, huh?" Stacy's voice was edgy. "Stop acting like I'm a horrible snob.

Or do I have to remind you that you're a techie and my friend at the same time?"

Tess snorted. "You don't know what it's like being a techie, Stacy. It's rough even for me, and since I'm a cheerleader, plenty of kids forget I'm a vo-tech major. But when the captain of the cheering squad starts dating an auto mechanics student—" She pulled her shoulders up almost to her ears, then let them drop again. "Kids like Dex and Val could make it rotten for you."

"I'm not worried about a few snobs," Stacy insisted airily. " 'Sticks and stones can break my bones . . .' and all that jazz. Why should anybody care who I go out with?"

"Why should anybody care if I go out with Dave Prentice or not?" Tess responded. "Remember, Stacy, you're the one who told me it mattered. And if you think it doesn't matter for you, good luck. Maybe you're right. Maybe you can get away with things a mere techie like myself could never dream of."

"Oh, techie, schmeckie! I can't believe anyone thinks that stuff's important anymore. It's like saying kids are going to jump all over Dennis's case for going out with a girl whose hair is shorter than his!"

"You don't think they will, do you?" Janet asked. "He'd just die!"

"Of course I don't think they will," Stacy replied firmly. "This is the twentieth century, isn't it? Anybody has a right to date anyone he or she wants. If a few spoiled brats don't like it, that's their problem. Anyhow," she added, pushing away her half-eaten tuna melt, "I don't think anybody's going to even notice who I'm dating. It's no big deal. Really, it's not!"

As the three other girls continued to stare at her in disbelief, she stood up and grabbed her tray and shoulder bag. Her idea of a good time certainly wasn't sitting there while her friends looked at her as if she'd just turned into Typhoid Mary. "Listen, I've got some things to look up in the library before next period. See you at practice, Tess."

"See you, Stace."

"'Bye, Stacy."

"Good luck."

What's luck got to do with it, she thought bitterly as she stormed across to the tray drop-off. Nothing like having your friends be the first to spoil the first good thing that had happened to your life.

She couldn't expect them to understand, though. Not even her best friend thought Stacy Harcourt had the right to be bored or dissatisfied with any facet of her charmed existence. They couldn't see that Nick had made all the difference in the world to her drab life.

TEN

For the rest of the week, Stacy was too occupied with thoughts of Nick to care whether her classmates approved of him or not. Nothing could come between them. They had different backgrounds, different friends, different interests, but those differences were exactly what made their relationship fascinating. And their interest in each other was something they shared deeply.

The electricity that had been so powerful the moment they met only fed itself and grew stronger. They would pass in the corridors and a shiver would course down Stacy's spine. Nick would phone, and the huskiness of his unmistakable voice would make her feel so weak she'd have to sit down. They'd brush against each other, and her skin would tingle for hours afterward. The chemistry between them was deliciously, dangerously explosive.

Not that it was simply a matter of chemistry. The world Nick introduced Stacy to was so different, she was naturally intrigued. Nick's world was vital, gutsy, the real thing. She was fascinated by everything about him.

On Saturday, Stacy met Nick's sister, Cora. Thin and pale, with dark hair pulled back in a plastic barrette, she astonished Stacy with her ability to care for two active babies, cook at the stove, and keep up a running stream of conversation.

Cora seemed capable and earthy, grown-up compared to the girls Stacy knew. And to think she'd graduated from high school the same year as Stacy's sister, Sarah!

"I'll bet you're Sarah Harcourt's kid sister," Cora said when Nick took Stacy to lunch at the cramped prefab bungalow Cora shared with her husband, Arnie, and their children. "You look just like her."

"You know my sister?" As soon as the words were out, Stacy prayed she hadn't sounded shocked. But she couldn't imagine her sister and Cora being acquainted.

"Sure. We graduated together. Oh, I don't mean we were great buddies or anything like that. You know, Sarah was one of those girls who was always worrying about getting into college and what she was going to major in and stuff like that. Not me." She laughed wryly. "Arnie and I knew from the time we were in tenth grade we'd be getting married someday. Probably wouldn't have waited till graduation if my folks hadn't put their foot down. Not like Nick here. He's too smart to settle down too fast."

Stacy blinked at that. How could his own sister think of Nick as somebody's husband? He was just a kid!

"You like chili?" Cora went on without missing a beat. "I made up some chili for lunch. That's Arnie's favorite, and this way he can have a big bowl for supper when he finishes his shift."

"Where does your husband work?" Stacy asked, interested in anything that was connected with Nick.

"Out at Geeson's Mill on the Interstate. He'll probably make foreman next year or the next, and then we can move to a bigger place, where I'll have some room to move around." She laughed as her little girl, who was about a year and a half, almost tripped her by grabbing onto her shins. "C'mon, Cammy, give Mommy some room, huh?"

"She's adorable," Stacy said warmly, studying the family resemblance in the toddler's big brown eyes and the shock of rich brown curls so like Nick's.

"Isn't she a cutie?" Nick asked. "She's going to be a real heartbreaker when she grows up."

"Oh, she's a cutie, all right." Cora beamed with motherly adoration. "But it's easy for Nick to say. He doesn't have to spend the whole day with her. She can run me ragged. Some days nap time doesn't roll around soon enough. We named her Camille, after that old movie with Greta Garbo, you know. But we just call her Cammy all the time. When she grows up, though, she'll be Camille, and she'll be glad she's got a pretty name. Not like Cora."

Nick broke in, chuckling. "Mom insisted on naming us all after her sisters and brothers. Lucky for me one brother's my uncle Nick."

"Camille's a beautiful name. It's so romantic, isn't it? What about your little boy? What's his name?" She gestured toward the playpen that was taking up a good third of the small, square living room, where a dark-haired baby in blue corduroy rompers had pulled himself to a standing position and was clinging to the bars.

"That's Chuckie. He's just nine months, so he can't walk much on his own yet. But, boy, you should see him crawl. He could win the Olympic crawling marathon! That's why I try to keep him in the playpen as much as possible. I keep worrying that I'll step smack on him one day. He's that fast, under your feet before you can even see him coming."

As if he knew he was the topic of conversation, the baby sprang into action, alternately shaking the bars of the playpen and lifting up his arms and shrieking, telling the world he wanted out.

Cora didn't pause. She just picked Chuckie up and balanced him on one hip while she dished up the chili and took garlic bread out of the oven, casually ignoring the little girl who never loosened her hold on Cora's slacks. Stacy was pleased to see that Nick jumped in to help without Cora's asking, taking a jug of iced tea from the refrigerator and filling their glasses.

"Your sister's amazing," she told Nick after they'd left and were heading out toward Watson's Grove. "I don't know how she does it."

"Yeah, she's something, isn't she?" he said with admiration. "Sometimes that little house is like a three-ring circus, but Cora hardly ever loses her cool."

Stacy's own sister was still just a schoolgirl, three years older than she was, and there was Cora, already busy raising a family and taking care of a household, occupied with the real business of life. It made Stacy feel immature and frivolous. What was the biggest commitment in her life—cheerleading?

If she was wholeheartedly impressed by Nick's sister, Stacy found she had mixed feelings about the speedway. The races were thrilling enough, but she was on the edge of her seat in the bleachers watching the cars spin and squeal around the track, cringing when one would smack into another with a sickening metallic crunch.

"How can you actually like to race?" she shouted to Nick over the revving of the engines and the cheers and catcalls of the throng. "I'd be terrified!"

"Sure, sometimes you're scared," Nick answered happily. "But that's half the fun. You're proving yourself every minute you're down there in your car. And nothing beats the way you feel when you win. It's like being king of the world!"

As they watched one stock-car driver being presented with a championship cup, Stacy realized she'd rarely seen anyone so flushed with triumph, so ecstatic. In spite of the grime and perspiration that ran down his weather-beaten face, the winner looked as if this was the happiest day of his life.

And that's just what he said in his jubilant sentence of acceptance: It was the happiest day of his life. Stacy imagined herself standing by as Nick was presented with a gilt trophy. *How proud I'd be*, she thought. These men were celebrities to the fans cheering them on. They were stars, heroes.

She was still impressed later when they walked around the pits where men in coveralls worked on cars with wrenches, screwdrivers, and oilcans. They all greeted Nick with the familiarity of an old friend, and even though a few of them looked older than some of the teachers at school, they treated Nick as an equal.

There was an undercurrent of excitement in the pit area that gave Stacy goose bumps. "Did you catch Big Al's crack-up last week?" one man asked Nick. "Went right into the wall at the far end of the track. I really thought he was done for, man, but that guy's lucky. He walked away without a scratch."

Another remarked, "Won't be seeing you for a few weeks, Cooper. I'm leaving tomorrow for California. Driving out for the heats in the big race at Ontario Speedway there. I figure I've got a good chance of qualifying."

These people traveled more from one race to the next each year than she had traveled in her life. And Nick knew and was known by some real pros. Stacy listened spellbound as Nick talked to one driver who had just raced in France and another recently back from two years on the Italian circuit. It wasn't just thrilling. Racing was glamorous!

After touring the pits, they climbed into the car. Stacy was beginning to share Nick's affection for it. As she kissed Nick and held him tight, the racetrack and lunch at Cora's began to fade from Stacy's mind. Soon she wasn't aware of anything but the two of them. The silky texture of his hair twined through her fingers, the electrified reaction of her skin as his hand slid beneath her sweater at the back of her waist, the softness of his lips that gave way to the harshness of their mingled breathing as it grew heavier and more intense—this was the world, the entire world, for the time they were locked in each other's embrace.

When his hand slid around to the front of her sweater, she pushed him away. "No, Nick," she whispered, her voice and her lips trembling.

"Mmmmm," he murmured, burying his lips in her neck. "You really do something to me, Stacy. You taste so good, you feel so good."

"You, too," she gasped. Then, as the electricity began flooding through her again, she pushed him away once more, a bit more forcefully this time.

"Whoa!" She giggled shakily, sliding out of his grasp and closer to the passenger side of the car. "I've got to catch my breath."

"Tell me about it!" He chuckled, slouching down farther in the seat and throwing back his head. "Whew! I feel like I've just run a four-minute mile." Reaching across the seat, he took her hand and lifted it to his chest. "Here, feel my heart."

Beneath her fingertips, she felt the strong, rapid beating. Nick's blood was pumping in double time: there was something magical in feeling his heart throbbing beneath her touch and in knowing she was the one to have caused his excitement.

He moved her hand from his chest to his lips, tenderly kissing the tips of her fingers. "You drive me crazy, you know." He groaned. "Wow!"

"The chemistry between us is—" she began, then stopped and laughed. "All I can say is that if chemistry *class* were like this, I'd be getting straight A's."

"I know what you mean," he agreed softly,

kissing her fingers once more before setting her hand back on her own lap and releasing it. "You're something else, Stacy."

"You, too, Nick."

He leaned over and kissed her again, gently this time. Now that their breathing was back to normal, it was quiet inside the car. "I'd better drop you off at home. Even though I had the day off, I promised Uncle Joe I'd stop by and help him rebuild a carburetor on someone's truck."

"On your day off?" Stacy didn't try to hide her disappointment. She'd taken it for granted that she and Nick would be spending the whole evening together.

He started the car. "See, it's pretty complicated, rebuilding a carburetor. It's different with every different kind of engine. Different kits and so on. It's one job where I can use all the practice I can get if I want to get it right. So it was no sweat to tell my uncle I'd put in a couple of hours with him." He smiled. "Not that I wouldn't rather be with you."

That made her feel better. "We'll have plenty of time to be together," she said hopefully.

"You mean it, don't you?" he asked, his voice hushed with wonder. "You really don't care that I'm a techie?"

"You don't care that I'm a cheerleader, do you?"

"Of course I don't care that you're a cheerleader! Any guy in his right mind would want to be with you, Stacy."

"I happen to think that any girl in her right mind would feel this way about you," Stacy retorted, smiling. "So if you don't care that I'm a cheerleader, why should I care that you're a techie?"

"C'mon, it's different, and you know it."

"It's no different to me," she insisted. "I don't like or not like you because you're a techie. I like you because you're Nick Cooper. Period."

"You're terrific, you know that? I must be the luckiest guy in all of Midvale."

"You are. And just make sure you don't forget it," she teased, and they both laughed.

It took real effort for her to get out of the car instead of throwing herself back into Nick's arms. Even after he pulled away, her legs threatened to fold beneath her in melting weakness as she walked up the path and into the house.

Her mother looked up from the piece of needlepoint she was working on as Stacy entered the living room. "Back already, dear? I thought you'd be out for the evening."

"Nope, I'm in for the night. But I had a wonderful day, just wonderful!"

"That's nice, dear," Mrs. Harcourt said absentmindedly. Then she again looked up from the piece of canvas in her hands, and when she spoke, her voice was sharper. "Whatever did

Rich do to his car? It sounded like a jet taking off when he drove away."

"Different car. Different date. I'm not seeing Rich anymore, Mother."

"Oh? I thought you two got along so well together. Who's the lucky boy this time?"

"His name is Nick Cooper, and he's the most fabulous boy in the universe!"

"Don't gush, dear," her mother said mildly. "I do think your father and I should meet this Nick, especially in view of his idea of transportation."

Her parents were certain to like Nick, Stacy told herself as she hurried upstairs and into her room. Her eyes fell on the glass block atop the dresser. "Tough luck, butterfly, but I'm not like you anymore," she said out loud. "I'll never feel trapped again."

Nick has opened a whole new world to me, she thought as she remembered Watson's Grove, Cora, Jimmy, and Margie. Everything was perfect now, as perfect as her beautiful butterfly. Only better. Because, unlike the butterfly, her feeling for Nick was living, changing, growing.

ELEVEN

It was just two weeks later that Dex Grantham pinned her against the wall of the second-floor science corridor between second and third periods, drawling, "Well, if it isn't Miss Blond-and-Beeeeyoootiful. I missed you at Tif's party after the game Saturday."

Stacy snickered, but she wished Dex would just get lost. She'd had no interest in Tif Rafferty's party, and she didn't think twice before telling Nick she'd be able to go over to Jimmy's for dinner instead. If it had been one of Valerie's parties, she might have felt different, since missing one of those was never a good idea, not with Val's acid tongue always ready to wag. But missing Tif's party wasn't a crisis, especially since her parents were always present to make sure no one danced too closely or played music too loudly. A party like that was a world apart from the last few Stacy had attended with Nick.

Among Nick's friends, parties were a real reason to celebrate, and Stacy knew the partying went on long after she and Nick had to leave. Of course, those parties were grown-up affairs, not silly, high-school gatherings.

Stacy pushed gently against Dex's arm. "Is this a trick to get me to admire your muscles?"

"Devastating, aren't they?" He winked, but he didn't move to let her pass. "So how come you skipped Tif's?"

"If you really must know, I had something better to do," she retorted. "I know it's hard for you to imagine anybody could have anything better to do than worship at your feet. Of course, if I had known for sure you'd be there, I might have changed my plans," she added sweetly, not wanting to be too caustic with Dex.

"Well, tell me, babe, have I blown my big shot with you by choosing premed instead of the local garage?"

"If you're trying to find out if I'm seeing Nick Cooper, the answer is yes. Now, do you want to let me go?"

He laughed as she walked away, then called after her, "No hard feelings, gorgeous! Just remember, any time you get tired of taking a walk on the wild side, I'm available!"

What a dope Dex could be, Stacy fumed as she kept on walking, smiling into the curious stares of the other kids who passed. If Dex Grantham thought he was going to embarrass her, he had another think coming!

Well, the heck with Dex and everyone like him, Stacy thought as she turned into her classroom.

Why wouldn't kids who didn't know the first thing about how real people lived make snide remarks? Nick had twice as much going for him as most of the guys at Midvale, so why should she try to hide her relationship with him? From now on, anybody who invited her anyplace could expect to see Nick Cooper, too.

At lunch that day she tried to tell Tess and Gina what Dex had said, certain they'd understand. But to her surprise, Gina was silent after Stacy had said what a lot of nerve Dex had, and Tess practically took Dex's side.

"How come you *didn't* go to Tif's party?" she asked quietly. "It was fun, really, and plenty of kids asked where you were."

"Because I didn't *want* to go to Tif Rafferty's party," Stacy explained patiently. "We'd already been asked to have dinner with Nick's friends."

"Was that so much more fun than being with your own friends?" Tess asked.

"Oh, for Pete's sake, of course not!" Stacy hesitated. "No, maybe it was. I mean, if you've been to one of Tif Rafferty's parties, you've been to 'em all. You just didn't know that because you'd never been invited before."

"Thanks, Stacy," Tess muttered. "Why don't you rub it in?"

"Would you stop being so sensitive?" Stacy's voice rose in frustration. "All I mean is that it's new to you. I think it's great that Valerie's decided you can be on her friends' party lists now that you and Dave are serious. I wasn't

125

trying to put you down. All I meant is that I wouldn't have had as much fun as I had with Margie and Jimmy."

"I think everybody guessed that when you didn't show up." Tess's voice was even.

"Are we going to work on that new paired-off routine today?" Gina broke in before Stacy and Tess had a chance to start a real argument.

"At practice, you mean?" Stacy sent Gina a silent look of appreciation for getting her out of what could have turned into a nasty scene.

Gina nodded. "You said we should all learn the words of the cheer by today, so I figured we'd be working on it."

"Oh, sure, sure," Stacy assured her, mentally kicking herself. She'd completely forgotten about the intricate new twosome routine she and Ms. Bowen had created. Now she'd have to try to learn all the words and the sequences by the time the last bell rang.

"Well, we're going to go get some extra practice out on the lawn," Tess said, standing. "I don't suppose you want to come along, do you?"

"Not really. I told Nick I'd meet him for a minute or two up on the third floor when his class lets out, so I want to get up there early." Stacy might have added that she didn't want to risk having to practice the new cheer, since she hadn't learned it yet.

She really meant to memorize the cheer perfectly in study hall that afternoon, but as she flipped open her notebook, a racing magazine Nick had loaned her slipped out and she was caught up in that instead. Nick was so pleased when she acted as if she cared about racing.

As a result, cheering practice was worse than she'd ever thought it could be.

The first half was all right, since Stacy made sure she called for cheers she knew by heart and could get through with her eyes closed. For a while, she thought she'd be able to put off the new routine until the next practice. Then Ms. Bowen said clearly, "Weren't you planning to do some work on that new partner routine today, Stacy?"

"Whoops, that's right," she agreed, trying to make it seem as if it had just slipped her mind. "Okay, gang, let's pair off the same way we did last week. Next time, we'll work on alternate partners."

Each pair consisted of a junior and a senior: Gina and Kathy, Tess and Patricia, and Stacy and Sherri. She'd chosen Sherri as her partner because the other girl was the best junior on the squad, and Stacy had figured Sherri's skill would show off her partner as well. Now she wished she hadn't been so quick to grab the limelight for herself. As soon as they started, Sherri's expertise made Stacy look halfhearted and unprepared.

Stacy tried to get by with mouthing the words, shouting loudly during the parts she could remember and hoping the sound of the others would cover for her when she forgot. She might have succeeded with that ploy if she hadn't blown the physical part of the routine. She was the only one who did a split jump (and a flabby one at that) when everybody else executed precision-timed back jumps in perfect arches. And when it came time for her to bend her knees and support Sherri, who was standing in an arch on them, she overbalanced and almost fell over backward. If Sherri hadn't shifted her weight rapidly, they both would have fallen in a heap on the hardwood floor.

"Is something wrong, Stacy?" Ms. Bowen's voice was more cool than concerned after they'd run through the whole routine. "You did know we were doing this cheer today, didn't you?"

"Yes, I did. And I thought I had it," she fibbed. "Maybe I'm just a little nervous today."

Ms. Bowen looked skeptical. Stacy wished she could have come up with a better excuse on the spur of the moment. After all, who could believe Stacy Harcourt would get nervous about cheering—and at nothing but a practice session?

"Maybe we should go through the singles part of the cheer one at a time so you girls can critique each other," Ms. Bowen suggested. "I'm sure hearing the other girls do the cheer will refresh your memory, Stacy," she added dryly.

The six of them sat on the bottom bench of the bleachers while Ms. Bowen stood off to the side, calling their names one by one. Stacy went last, but she was afraid she didn't do much better than she had with Sherri—worse, probably, because there were no other voices to cover up her mistakes.

"All right," Ms. Bowen said when they'd finished. "Any suggestions for Gina?"

Naturally, everyone shook her head at that. Gina's jumps were always top quality.

"What about Tess?"

"Well," Sherri began hesitantly, since the cheerleaders usually hated to criticize one another too harshly, "it was no big thing, but on her second split jump, her right leg was quite a bit higher than her left."

"Good point," Ms. Bowen said, and Tess nodded solemnly. "Just work on pulling that left leg up as you push off the ground.

"How about Kathy?"

Kathy came in for a bit more criticism, but that was expected, since she was new to cheering this year and didn't have as much strength in her legs as the others. Since she was happy to be on the squad, she welcomed all the constructive criticism she could get.

"And Patricia?"

Stacy thought, as captain, she should make some remark just so they'd see she'd paid attention and knew her business. "A couple of times her back jump veered to the right," she put in. "Her feet were just a little over to the side."

"And your voice sort of fades out when you jump, Patricia," Gina put in, her tone gentle. "Try to take an extra-big breath before you spring up."

"Good suggestion, Gina. Now, how about Stacy?" the coach asked, and Stacy felt everyone look at her and then quickly look away. "Well?" Ms. Bowen prompted when nobody said a word.

"Wellll," Gina said slowly, "I thought some of her jumps could have been higher."

Well, she'd expected some criticism from Gina. After all, didn't she have her eye on the winter captaincy? No one else said a word at first, and Stacy was about to get to her feet to announce the end of practice when Sherri spoke up. "She lost the beat once or twice."

"Was that because you didn't know the words, Stacy?" Ms. Bowen asked sharply.

"I don't know why they slipped my mind." She repeated her feeble lie in a muffled voice, wanting to ask Ms. Bowen why the coach was picking on her. Hadn't she already admitted she didn't have the words of the cheer memorized yet?

"She missed a sequence," Tess piped up. "Just like the first time, she did a split jump when it should have been a back jump."

"And her split jump was awfully low," Patricia chimed in. "Not much extension on it."

"Isn't the kick in the marching part supposed to be higher?" Kathy asked in a tiny voice, as if she was afraid to criticize the captain. *C'mon*, Stacy thought, *don't be shy, Kathy. Go for my throat like everyone else.*

By the time Ms. Bowen dismissed practice

and she was walking to her car, Stacy was in a foul mood. She couldn't believe the pettiness of the other girls, especially Tess. Since she'd been so busy keeping the line free at home in case Nick called her from the garage at night, she and Tess hadn't really talked for what seemed like ages. She'd been looking forward to walking out to the lot with Tess, maybe even stopping for a soda before heading home.

But she didn't get a chance to even suggest getting together. As soon as practice ended, Tess and Patricia started buzzing together, their heads close and their voices lowered as they sat down on the bottom row of bleachers. It was clear to Stacy that she wasn't wanted there.

Sherri and Kathy scurried out together, with Sherri calling back, "Got to run. We're hitting that big sale out at the mall before we go home."

"Well, don't bother asking me if I'd like to come along," Stacy muttered under her breath, although she'd never sought out the company of the junior cheerleaders before. A senior who spent her time with juniors risked looking as if she couldn't find any seniors willing to be friends. *Obviously, Tess isn't worried about* that, Stacy observed with a sniff.

Gina was talking solemnly to Ms. Bowen. *Probably worried about her routine for the stupid election*, Stacy thought scornfully. As if someone as insecure and self-conscious as Gina had a chance of wresting the captainship away from her!

Well, I welcome the competition, Stacy assured herself as she slammed her car door and roared out of the parking lot. A little competition couldn't hurt her, nor could a few cold shoulders. She'd look at these things as mere challenges to be overcome.

I'm perfectly happy being here alone, anyhow, she told herself when she was ensconced in her room. It looked so different now, much hipper and less prissy with the Bjorn Borg poster stripped from the wall and rolled up in her closet.

The only thing that kept Stacy from being ecstatic was Nick's heavy work schedule. She didn't get to see him nearly as much as she'd have liked. In a way, though, she supposed that made the moments they shared even more precious. And she really liked going over to the garage and spending time with him on Saturdays and sometimes after school. She'd have gone every single day if she hadn't been sure Nick's Uncle Joe would get annoyed. But she liked Cooper's Garage, with its pungent aromas of motor oil, hot metal, and gasoline. She especially liked watching Nick as he tinkered with the cars, his hair tousled, forehead wrinkled in concentration, hands sure and swift with a wrench or tire iron or hydraulic jack.

Nick enjoyed teaching her about cars, too. In a short time, she'd already learned the difference between a Phillips screwdriver and a regular one, knew all the different gas additives and what they did, and could probably change her own oil if she ever felt like doing it.

Nick seemed to like spending any spare time he had at the Harcourts, and though Stacy was sure from hints they'd dropped that her parents would be happier if she wasn't tied up so much with the boy they continually referred to as "your mechanic," Mr. and Mrs. Harcourt didn't seem to actively dislike Nick and were always pleasant to him.

As much as Nick seemed to like visiting Stacy's home, she suspected he was more attracted by the things in it than by the fact that it was her house. Even though he acted as if the VCR were commonplace for him, he played with it like a little kid with an electronic game, hitting the freeze-frame and instant-replay buttons until Stacy was ready to scream.

Not that Nick admitted his attraction. It was the way he kept referring to things that told her he was intrigued. "A telephone next to the toilet," he'd say each time he returned from the first-floor powder room. "I'll tell you, Stacy, sometimes I think your folks are weird!"

For her part, Stacy found that she was getting used to the guys who hung out at the Grove. The more she showed up there at Nick's side, the more they took her for granted and the less they leered at her when she walked by.

It didn't take long for her to realize that Nick Cooper was respected by these older guys, who'd often stop him to ask for advice about their engines. Nick was considered someone with a future in stock-car racing. He was still too young to qualify professionally, but he registered for local teen-amateur sprints.

When there was an amateur sprint at the Grove one Saturday afternoon, Stacy sat in the stands watching Nick's car roar by, her body rigid with fear for him. Cora sat on one side of her and Margie on the other; she didn't even realize how nervous she'd been until the flag dropped at the finish line, and they held up her palms to show where her nails had dug in.

"You'll get used to it," Margie told her. "You'll relax more with every race."

Stacy barely heard her. Her terror was already forgotten in exhilaration. Nick had finished second, edged out only by an older, more seasoned driver; and the cheers that echoed around her when his name was announced made her flush with pride. Nick was a hero to this crowd, and Stacy could bask in his glory.

Now that she knew Margie better, Stacy cringed when she remembered how intimidated she'd been by the other girl the first night she'd met her. Margie just tried to look older in order to be comfortable with Jimmy's crowd, most of whom were in their twenties. And although Margie had dropped out of school, she was as bright as the students in Stacy's classes. Stacy was trying to convince her to go to night school for her diploma.

Most important to Stacy, Margie had known

Nick for two years. Stacy could talk about Nick without Margie getting bored or responding as if Stacy were crazy—which was how she was sure her friends from Midvale would react if she tried discussing her boyfriend with them.

Of course, she knew better than to confide in a bunch of silly schoolkids. They couldn't begin to understand her feelings for Nick. To them, he was just another techie.

Even the ones who didn't actually make snippy remarks or outright slurs cut Stacy dead when she brought up Nick's name. Tess and Gina spent almost every lunch hour now practicing their cheer routines for the election, so Stacy usually sat with Janet and Marsha.

One Monday, Janet talked endlessly about how she and Dennis Callahan had spent the past Saturday, not particularly interesting news, since they had spent almost every Saturday together for two months. Marsha was listening so closely she might have been recording Janet's every word—interrupting every now and then to relate some anecdote about her and Wayne and their weekend.

"I had a pretty good time Saturday myself," Stacy finally cut in, when it appeared neither girl was going to ask.

Both girls turned to her, looking almost surprised that she was still there. "Oh, what did you do?" Janet asked. "Go visit Sarah at school?"

"No. She's coming home next weekend, as a

135

matter of fact. Saturday Nick and I went out to the Grove to watch his friend Jimmy race. You should have seen it!" she enthused, her eyes shining more at the memory of sitting in the bleachers wrapped in Nick's strong arms than at the recollection of the competition. "It was really something."

"Oh?" Janet sounded indifferent.

"That must have been fun." Marsha's voice was flat with lack of interest.

Then Janet's shorn hair and Marsha's tawny waves swung away from her, and the girls continued their conversation as if Stacy had never spoken.

Stacy felt like leaving the lunchroom then and there, but she still had half her lunch left to eat. She vowed not to be as rude as they had been. She murmured and nodded as if all she was hearing were fascinating, even though she privately believed a boy like Dennis, with all his activities and school projects, was stiflingly juvenile.

When Stacy saw Tess later in the day, she remarked, "Too bad you didn't get to lunch. Janet and Marsha were having the most fascinating conversation about their boyfriends. I was afraid I'd die of boredom before I finished my chicken à la king."

She expected Tess to laugh in agreement. Instead, the other girl shook her head. "Come on, Stacy, you're starting to sound like Valerie Masters. It's not Janet and Marsha's problem if you suddenly find them boring." Then, before Stacy had a chance to retort, she asked, "How come you aren't practicing for the cheering election yet? Are you still working on your routine?"

"Now you're starting to sound like Gina," Stacy snapped. "Of course I'm not working up a routine yet. I mean, what's the big deal? The election's not for a couple of weeks yet."

"I thought cheering mattered to you," Tess said quietly, looking puzzled.

"Of course cheering matters to me! Who said it didn't? I show up for all the practices, don't I? You know being captain of the squad is the most important thing in my life, Tess."

"Is it? Funny, it seems as if you can't be bothered to concentrate at practice anymore—and the only time you've been enthusiastic at a game lately was two weeks ago when Nick managed to come."

"You're imagining things," Stacy said firmly. "I'm very serious about cheering, and you know it. And what's so strange about my being happy because Nick could come to a game? Just because Dave's at every game, you've got no idea what it's like for me. You shouldn't just think of yourself, Tess," she added gently. What was happening to her friends? Even Tess was growing rude and thoughtless.

Tess's answer shocked her. "*I* shouldn't just think of *myself*?" She snorted. "That's really rich, Stacy. And if you're smug because you think you've got the winter captainship all sewn up, you might change your mind if you bother to think about it for five minutes."

"What's that supposed to mean? That you and Gina have worked up such terrific routines you're going to edge me out? So what? Listen, Tess, if somebody else wins the election, more power to her. I don't think you believe for a second that I can't come up with a dynamite cheer, anyhow." Anger flooded through Stacy. "You want to know what I do think? I think you've been acting uptight ever since I started dating Nick. I thought you'd gotten over that a while ago. But obviously you're still mad because Nick wanted to go out with me and not you."

"Don't be ridiculous!" Tess snapped right back at her. "Oh, I'm sure you went out of your way to get a date with Nick, which I didn't appreciate, since you never would have noticed him if I hadn't been interested. But I was never *seriously* interested in him, Stacy. No more than you are."

"You've got no idea what you're saying," Stacy argued. "Okay, so maybe I did go out of my way to see Nick again after we'd met. But that was only so you wouldn't lose a wonderful guy like Dave. And as far as my not being really interested in Nick, that's absurd. Nick's the only thing that even comes close to cheering in my life."

"You can spare me the garbage about how

you were trying to save me by grabbing Nick for yourself," Tess said dryly. "And as far as Nick meaning so much to you, it'll be interesting to see if you feel the same way after you get tired of flaunting your relationship with him in front of the whole school and start actually *having* a relationship with him."

"And just what," Stacy asked, "is that supposed to mean?"

"It means I wonder how fascinating you'll find Nick after losing the cheering-captain election," Tess retorted. "Maybe the novelty will wear a little thin then."

"Why are you picking on me like this?" Stacy asked, genuinely hurt. "I thought we were supposed to be friends, Tess. You actually sound as if you want me to lose!"

"We are friends," Tess said, her voice kinder. "Or at least we were. It's just that—well, sometimes I feel I don't know you anymore, Stacy. You've changed so much."

Tess paused, and Stacy waited for her to say more. But the harsh clanging of the bell put an end to their conversation. "Look, I've got to run," Tess told her. "We'll talk about this some other time okay?"

"Sure," Stacy agreed. Secretly, she was relieved to be able to hurry away down the hallway in the opposite direction from Tess.

She'd been shaken by what the other girl had said. Tess's accusations were groundless, and Stacy attributed them to her original theory that Tess was jealous of her success with Nick. It was absurd to suggest she was a different person just because she now preferred being a spectator at the racetrack to sitting around trading gossip in a pizza parlor. She had simply grown beyond Nicola's. After all, since Tess had started seeing more of Dave, she didn't spend so much time with the big groups, either.

What had shocked Stacy was Tess's insinuation that she was in definite peril of losing the cheering-squad captaincy. She had never considered the possibility that she would be replaced, and she was astonished to learn that someone else had. Cheering wouldn't be the same to her if Gina or Tess became captain. That would be the same as a demotion!

It was Nick, Stacy sadly realized, who'd placed her in jeopardy. That speech Tess had recited about Stacy's not practicing for the election hadn't fooled her for a second. The captaincy had to do with popularity, not skill.

And falling for Nick had placed her in danger of losing her popularity.

There was a simple solution, Stacy realized as she dashed into her next class to the clang of the late bell. All she would have to do to secure her popularity was break up with Nick. Once the words spread that Stacy had given up her flirtation with the wrong kind of boy, once she showed that being part of the right crowd meant more to her than her relationship with a techie, she'd be on top in Midvale High again.

But Stacy Harcourt would never give in like a coward. She'd never been a quitter, and she wasn't about to become one now. She couldn't imagine life without Nick. Those moments spent in his arms, his lips on hers, were what made the rest of her life bearable.

There had to be a way to hang on to both Nick and the captaincy. All she had to do was find it.

TWELVE

"No, Nick, please . . . I can't . . . *Don't do that!*"

Struggling to get her breath back, Stacy hurled Nick away, pushing with all her strength against his chest. Not trusting herself to speak, she faced forward, staring out across the red flames on the Trans Am's hood at the reflection of the nearly full moon in Brinton's Lake. "Why do you want me to do something I'd be ashamed of?" she asked, fighting tears. "Why does our being together always have to end in a battle?"

"I'm sorry, Stacy, honest I am," Nick said, and his voice was so thick with emotion she was afraid he was in danger of crying, too. "I don't know what comes over me. But I know it's not just me," he added defensively. "Admit it, Stacy. You always want to go further, too. That's why you don't stop me before you do."

"Sometimes I hate being seventeen!" she exclaimed passionately. "It's not fair, wanting to do things you know you're too young to handle.

And we are too young, Nick. At least, I know I am. I don't think I could deal with waking up in the morning knowing I'd gone too far the night before."

"I know." He sighed. "And I probably wouldn't like myself much if I pressured you into it. But how long are we supposed to keep parking here and just—just necking?" he asked, his usually deep voice tight and angry.

She was silent for a while. Outside, the lake and sky were still and peaceful, but Stacy, normally so cool and controlled, fought against her churning emotions.

Finally, her tone heavy with defeat, she said, "Maybe we shouldn't park so much. Maybe we should find other things to do."

"Like what?" he groaned. "Hang out at Nicola's all night or go to the sock hop in the gym? You know that kind of stuff leaves me cold."

What does he want me to say? Stacy asked herself. *What more can I do?*

She was weary of the noise and sameness of Watson's Grove, but she couldn't tell Nick that. She had sacrificed Nicola's, victory hops, and double-dating with her old friends because she knew those activities would make Nick uncomfortable. She had no other solution. And yet they had to find other outlets for their energy besides parking. Their passions were too strong. As tired as Stacy had become of stock-car races and loud, raucous parties, her longing for Nick only grew more intense.

"Maybe we should both try to think about it," she suggested feebly.

"Let's get out of here for now," Nick said tautly, starting the car. "I can't be shut up with you like this without wanting to grab you and—"

"I know." She cut him off, not wanting to hear what he'd like to do, since she was filled with the same desires. If they kept on talking, she was afraid she would give in.

By the time the Trans Am halted in front of Stacy's house, Nick had regained his composure. "I'll call you tomorrow night when I get back from Indiana, okay?" he said.

Stacy just nodded. She'd looked forward to spending part of Sunday with Nick, but Nick had promised to work on the pit crew for a friend at an Indiana race. *Besides*, Stacy told herself as she walked up to the front door, *it isn't as if I have nothing to do tomorrow.* Her sister had arrived home for the weekend late Friday evening. By the time Stacy had come home from her date with Nick that night, Sarah had already gone to bed, and Saturday she'd seen her so briefly it hadn't even counted. With an afternoon game to cheer at and a date with Nick as soon as he'd closed the garage, she hadn't saved a lot of free time.

I want to spend some time with Sarah, Stacy thought as she climbed wearily into bed, even though she couldn't help but see her sister as immature and frivolous in comparison with Nick's sister, Cora.

Sarah, with a section of the Sunday paper open beside her, was already seated at the dining room table eating cornflakes and sipping tea when Stacy came down the stairs. She looked up from the paper as Stacy clomped into the room in her big shaggy slippers and flannel pajamas, her eyes still heavy with sleep. "Dad had to go into the office for a while, and Mother went along to do some shopping downtown. Emma's at the market, but there's a fresh pot of tea on the warming tray in the kitchen."

"Thanks," Stacy mumbled as she pushed through the swinging door to the kitchen, her voice thick and not fully awake.

After she'd returned, gulped down some orange juice, and swallowed half a mug of tea, she felt more alive. "Is Emma going to pick up Mother's birthday cake?" she asked.

"Uh-huh." Sarah folded the paper she'd been reading and looked up, and Stacy felt the momentary surge of jealousy she'd experienced before upon realizing that her sister was absolutely beautiful while she herself was merely pretty.

She studied Sarah, who was busy describing the beaded sweater she'd bought for their mother. Her features were so much like Stacy's—the same streaked tawny hair, blue eyes, and finely chiseled bone structure—but they all seemed better placed, more refined on Sarah. Her sister's looks were more sharply defined, while Stacy's seemed somehow unfinished. Even now, without makeup, Sarah looked ready to see anybody, while Stacy wouldn't have dared go out in public without eye liner, mascara, and blush.

"By the way"—the change in Sarah's tone marked a change in subject that caught Stacy's attention—"where did you find this new crowd you're hanging out with? I never thought I'd see you with a girl like the one who picked you up yesterday after the game. And your new boyfriend really amazed me. I mean, he's cute as all get out, but is he really your type?"

"So Margie wears a little too much makeup. So what?" Stacy asked tightly, wondering if her sister was turning out to be as narrow-minded as her friends from school. "And maybe Nick doesn't dress or act like a Grantham, but he's as good as they are. And he's the type who fits in anyplace."

"Is he?" Sarah sounded more curious than judgmental. "He didn't seem awfully comfortable while he and Margie were in the living room waiting for you to come down. He sat on the edge of the couch as if he'd be blamed for getting it dirty. And when I tried to make small talk so he'd relax, he just hemmed and hawed as if I were a cop trying to drag a confession out of him, and he wouldn't look at anything but the carpet."

"He's just shy, Sarah." She defended Nick. "A lot of the vo-tech students at Midvale didn't grow up exactly in the lap of luxury, you know. But then, I suppose you didn't get to know any techies when you were there."

Instead of taking offense, Sarah just laughed at her sister's accusatory tone. "Come on, Stacy, do you think you're the first person to make getting turned on by a techie into a social issue? As a matter of fact, I had a few dates with Jerry Birch when I was a junior."

"What happened?" Stacy asked, interested. "Did you drop him because the other kids made your life miserable?"

"Thanks for your faith in my principles," Sarah said dryly. "As a matter of fact, I did drop him, but not because I gave a darn about what anyone thought."

"How come, then?"

"It didn't take me long to realize we didn't have anything in common except physical attraction. He wanted to be an electrician—he is one now, I guess—and was hooked on karate movies. And I finally realized I was being snobbier by dating him than by not dating him."

"How's that?" Stacy's interest was piqued now.

Sarah hesitated. "I'm not sure I can explain it. You see, it didn't have anything to do with Jerry's being vo-tech or being from a poor family—his mom was a widow with six kids. Jerry fascinated me, not just because I thought he was gorgeous, but because I wasn't looking at his life realistically."

"Well, it's not like that with Nick and me," Stacy said firmly. But before she could say anything to give weight to her case, her sister went on.

"See, I thought everything about Jerry was exciting. It was like the lady and the outlaw, you know? But then I woke up and saw that for me it was a short-term thing, that I was fascinated by his friends and his interests. But to Jerry, it was for real. It was his life. He thought the things I cared about—going to school and becoming a lawyer, being a cheerleader, the school dances—were as weird as I thought his Bruce Lee movies were. I realized it was fairer to him to break it off and let him find a girl who didn't secretly see him as entertainment. I didn't want to make a fool of him or of myself just so I could shock the other kids with my new love."

"Well, Nick's not like that," Stacy insisted. "He's a very nice guy when you give him a chance. And he really cares about me."

"Jerry was a nice guy, too," Sarah said mildly. Then, perhaps noting the closed expression her sister's face was assuming, she changed the subject. "Is he a senior at Midvale?"

Stacy nodded. "In fact, his sister was in your graduation class. Her name was Cora Cooper then."

"Of course, I remember." Sarah closed her eyes as if to picture Nick's sister. "Shy and skinny, right? She looked as if a good strong wind would knock her over. She was a sweet girl. What's she up to these days?"

"She's married and has two kids," Stacy answered. "And a cute little house. You probably wouldn't recognize her anymore. She's so grown-up now."

If Sarah noticed the accusing note in her sister's voice, a note that silently added "and you're not" to Stacy's last sentence, she gave no hint of it. Instead she said simply, "That's right. Poor Cora. She'd had her heart set on nursing school, and she would have made a terrific nurse. But then—"

"Then what?"

"Then she decided she was too much in love to wait to get married. She and her boyfriend had a wedding right after graduation. He'd just graduated from some other school and had a job in a factory." Sarah shivered. "I feel bad for her, being stuck like that when she's so young."

"Well, Cora doesn't feel stuck," Stacy insisted. "She's very happy, and her children are adorable. And she says all she wanted to do was get married. So maybe you've got her confused with someone else."

Suddenly, Stacy was thoroughly bored with this discussion. Why was she always trying to defend her actions? Now it was her turn to change the subject—to Sarah and college. But the look on her sister's face assured Stacy that Sarah was indeed remembering Cora Cooper.

Had she taken Cora's happiness too much at face value? Was Cora someone who'd accepted her situation and was determined to make the best of it? Cora did spend a lot of time asking Stacy questions about Sarah and her college.

Cora must have been no older than Stacy when she'd decided to get married. And while Stacy admired Cora's courage and strength, she could not imagine being married or even contemplating marriage. She'd thought it was wonderful that Nick's sister was so grown-up for her age. Now she wondered how long she would survive if she didn't have Emma and her own room. Had Cora missed more than she was getting in return?

Cora clearly loved her children. But might she have been able to offer them a better life if she had held on to her dream of becoming a nurse? Stacy smiled as she listened to Sarah talk about her dorm's blind-date party. Perhaps she had judged her sister a little harshly. No one else in a long time had made her think about things she took for granted.

Stacy and Sarah spent the rest of the day together, wrapping their mother's gifts (Stacy had bought a leather belt in her mother's favorite and hard-to-find shade of cobalt blue) and helping to decorate for the birthday party, when two other couples would be joining the Harcourts for dinner.

As she and Sarah were working together, Stacy remembered how much she liked her sister's company. Sarah made her laugh as no one else could with stories about the girls in her sorority, late-night dorm popcorn feasts, and the guys on the next floor.

By the time the guests arrived, the Harcourt dining room looked like a stage set. Sarah had hung cardboard clouds and sky blue ribbon bows from the chandelier and draped the chairs with streamers of ice blue crepe paper. A blue linen tablecloth and matching napkins completed the color scheme. Finally, Sarah and Stacy, giggling, dressed in outfits to match the decor. "Do you think blue will still be Mom's favorite color after this evening?" Stacy asked as she buttoned Sarah's silk dress.

At dinner, Stacy saw her mother and father as if they had just returned from a long trip, and she reminded herself how lucky she was that this elegant, gentle woman and distinguished yet easygoing man were her parents. And she was glad they had friends like Jeff Davis, her father's law partner, and his wife, Marybeth, and Kirk and Janet Derby, her mother's best friend since high school, people who treated Sarah and Stacy as equals and included them in their conversations.

Stacy was almost startled when the telephone rang at eight-thirty, just after Emily Harcourt had opened her gifts and Emma had served the cake, ice cream, and coffee.

"It's your phone, Stacy," Emma announced. "Nick Cooper."

Stacy excused herself from the table. As she took the steps to her room two at a time, she wondered how to tell Nick she was happy to stay at home that evening, even though it was still early enough to snatch some time with him. Tonight, she wanted to devote every minute to her family.

The crackle of the line when she picked up the phone suggested she didn't need an excuse, and Nick's first words confirmed that. "Thought I should let you know I'm stuck over here," he told her, his voice thin and far away, as if he were more than thirty miles distant. "We ran into some cousins of Al's and they wanted us to have supper at their house. Now they're taking us to a party someplace. Al won the race, so he wants to celebrate a little."

"Oh, I understand," Stacy told him. "I miss you, but—well, I've been busy with my sister, so I guess I can live until tomorrow."

A loud click indicated that Nick was using a pay phone and that his time was almost up. "I've got to go," he said, his words running together. "I'll see you at school tomorrow."

Stacy hung up, feeling relieved. Nick had let her off the hook. She hadn't had enough time with Sarah to suit her—and she wanted to ask her for some pointers about her cheering routine for the election.

Sarah had been a talented cheering captain at Midvale, and she planned to audition for the pep squad at Chatham in the spring. Stacy wouldn't think of telling her sister what Tess had said. She wasn't about to let Sarah know the Harcourt popularity at Midvale was suffering—but she couldn't help being worried that the kids might blackball her because of Nick.

Stacy knew she couldn't bear the shame of spending the rest of the senior year as just another member of the cheering squad. Every time she performed, a thousand eyes would be upon her, the eyes of the students who had punished her for daring to defy the social code of Midvale High. But Sarah could help her win the election by working up a clever cheer routine for Stacy to master in the short time left to her.

Not that Stacy believed for a minute she'd win the election with her cheering. While she couldn't obviously neglect her cheerleading duties, this contest was really a battle of popularity. To come out ahead, Stacy had to devote herself to recapturing her position as the most sought-after friend and ally at Midvale. She would smile at everyone and be friendly and act as if each and every person in the corridors at school mattered dearly to her.

She had neglected the other kids lately, kids who had learned to depend on her for confirmation of their own status. She was willing to admit that. *But it isn't too late,* she told herself optimistically as she walked back down the stairs to rejoin her family. If she moved carefully and played the game correctly, the winter captaincy and Nick Cooper could both be hers.

THIRTEEN

Stacy was so busy the following week that she didn't have as much time for Nick as she'd have liked. All week long, she worked at lunch and in the evening to perfect the simple but lively combination of back jumps, splits, turns, and a strategically placed shimmy that Sarah had devised for her.

By Friday, she was eager to see him. In spite of her determination to cheer as well as she ever had, she wasn't going to give up Saturday night with Nick. This week's football game against Valencia was on Friday night, so she'd automatically reserved Saturday night for her boyfriend.

Stacy noticed that there was a definite chill in the air Friday morning. The most thrilling fall of her life was drawing to a close.

Most of the day passed as the rest of the week had. She made a conscious effort to spread her charm and good intentions around, traveling through the halls with a bright smile and a cheerful hello for everyone she knew.

At lunch she again worked on her cheering routine for the election. She had eliminated some of the more complicated steps and jumps that Sarah had choreographed. Her cheering had become a bit rusty in the months since she'd met Nick, but a few minor additions would keep people from noticing that her special cheer was made up of only the simplest, most basic moves.

By the time Stacy changed into her uniform for the rally that afternoon, she had begun to worry a little about not having seen Nick all day. She had taken it for granted that he would understand why she'd been preoccupied all week. She hadn't found an opportunity to talk to him since Sunday night, although he must have been busy, too, because her phone had been silent. But there was nothing she longed for more than to be in Nick's arms again on Saturday night.

Stacy spotted him way up in the gym bleachers before the rally began, looking as bored as the friends he was seated with. She made a mental note to remind Nick that he should try to look more enthusiastic, since he was going with the captain of the cheering squad. After all, a cheerleader's boyfriend was expected to show the same school spirit she did. She suspected that if pep rally attendance hadn't been required, Nick would just have skipped the whole thing.

Stacy focused her attention on the rally itself; today, though, she felt more as if she were playing the role of captain rather than actually being the captain. The other girls no longer seemed to look to her for guidance as they had so eagerly that first day of cheerleading practice. Once or twice she thought she saw Kathy Phillips glancing Gina's way to pace herself. Stacy was determined to remind the squad and the school who was captain. She put fire in her instructions and in her cheering.

When the time came for the new paired-off cheer, she took a deep breath, praying that the words would come to her. Any squad member who expected her to blow it would be disappointed.

"M-I-D-V-A-L-E,
The Midvale Mustangs are the
Team for me!"

So far, so good. She was cheering in perfect synchrony with the others, and she hadn't missed a beat on the series of seven jumps that went with the letters spelling out the name of the school.

"Mustangs really kick
And Mustangs really run.
They don't cool down
Till the game is won!"

The tricky part was coming up now, the part where she was paired off with Sherri to execute a series of double jumps—split jumps side by side while they had their backs to the other pairs of cheerleaders, then high jumps with their hands held in an arc above their heads—ending with the pose where Sherri jumped up on Stacy's knees and arched her back. Stacy smoothed down her skirt. She didn't want anyone, especially not the rest of the squad, to guess she was so nervous that her palms were sweating.

"Come on, Mustangs,
Put on a show.
Take that ball
And go, go, go!

Come on, Mustangs,
Don't be shy.
Midvale's the greatest.
Now show 'em all why!"

She finished triumphantly, Sherri balanced perfectly on her knees. As Sherri jumped down and the squad swung into the final cheer, Stacy grinned. A few of her jumps earlier on may not have been as good as those of the others, but she had finished in triumph. She smiled broadly and was pleased to see each of the girls return her smile.

When Stacy turned toward the bleachers to search for Nick's approving glance, he was gone. The cheerleaders left the gym floor through the door to the locker room, but Stacy hurried out without changing or stopping to discuss the performance with the other girls. As she rummaged through her hall locker for her weekend books, Valerie Masters paused to remind Stacy about her party the following evening.

"You can even bring that gorgeous gas jockey if you want," she said magnanimously, ignoring Stacy's frequent reminders that Nick worked at a garage and not a gas station. "Of course," Valerie purred, "we'll all expect to see you there, no matter what. The week before the cheering-captain election, a girl needs all the friends she can get, doesn't she?"

"Blackmailer," Stacy muttered under her breath, but only when Valerie was well out of earshot.

Stacy stalled as she collected her books, expecting Nick to appear at any moment, the dimple deepening in his cheek as he smiled down at her. But he failed to arrive, and she soon felt foolish, nervously switching her stack of books from the crook of one arm to the other.

Poor Nick, she thought as she walked toward the stairway that led down to the parking-lot door. She hadn't paid enough attention to him lately. Now he had concluded that she was too busy for him this week.

Her regret turned to relief when she spotted Nick leaning against her car. Even from a distance there was no mistaking his build.

"Hi!" She hurried up to him, stretching to

plant a kiss on his cheek. "Were you waiting long?" she asked.

When Nick didn't say anything right away, Stacy was filled with misgivings. Maybe he *was* miffed with her for not going out of her way to make time for him. She continued apologetically, "Listen, I know I've made myself pretty scarce this week, but with the cheering election coming up and all—well, I hope you understand." Nick remained silent. "Come on," she said flirtatiously, leaning into him. "Sit in the car and talk to me for a few minutes and I'll make it up to you."

To Stacy's astonishment, Nick slid away from her, his hands dug deep in his pockets, his eyes averted. "Hey, I'm not going to attack you or anything like that," she said, feeling suddenly self-conscious and awkward.

"I know you're not, Stacy."

She stared at him, mystified. His voice was hushed and he was smiling slightly. But it was a sad smile, a scary smile. Her stomach clenched in an awful premonition of disaster.

"We can't get in the car with you leaning against the door, you know." She'd tried to keep her voice light. Now she winced at the way it sounded, weak and whining, more like a plea than pleasantry.

"Um, I've got to get over to the garage." He stumbled over the words, continuing to avoid her questioning gaze. "But I had to talk to you before I left school. I've wanted to talk to you all week, but—"

"But I was too busy for you? Oh, Nick, I really am sorry about that!"

"That's not what I was going to say." He looked straight at her now, smiling without joy. "I was going to say that I was avoiding you. I was afraid to talk to you."

"Why?" she asked, her voice barely more than a whisper of fear.

"I couldn't think of a way to say what I had to say."

"I take it you've thought of one now," she said with a touch of her usual tartness.

He smiled, more warmly now. "I've always liked your spirit, Stacy. That's one of the first things I noticed about you. You've really got something special about you."

"Is that what you've been wanting to tell me?" she asked stiffly, knowing that whatever he had to say, that wasn't it.

He shook his head. Then, taking a deep, shuddering breath, he said bluntly, "I don't think we should see each other anymore, Stacy. It's—well, it's not good for you. I mean, I've heard all the talk around school. I know the kids resent you for turning your back on all your friends for a techie."

"Don't give me that, Nick Cooper," she said, her voice full of the spirit that had abandoned her moments before. "You can forget telling me you're about to do something for my own good, because it won't work. I told somebody the same thing myself not long ago, so I know it's garbage."

"It's not all garbage." His voice rose in his own defense. Then he looked away again. "But I guess a lot of it is. Look, Stacy, last week when I went to the races with Al, we spent some time with his cousins. I think I told you that. . . . Anyhow, I'd met this one cousin of his before. Her name's Betty Ann and she's a junior at Brownville. Both her brother and her cousin race, and—"

"And now you want to break up with me just because you went to one party with this girl? But that's crazy, Nick!" Stacy protested.

"It wasn't just the one party," Nick admitted. "I've seen her every night since then—I had some time off coming, and it's slow lately so I could take more time off without pay."

"So what are you saying? That you think you're in love with this Betty Ann Whatsherface and don't need me anymore?"

"I don't think I'm in love with her or anything, Stacy. I like her, that's all. But—" He broke off, slapping his forehead with the heel of one hand. "I don't even know how to say it. I guess I just have more fun with Betty Ann. Not that she's more fun than you are, Stacy," he added quickly. "She's not nearly as pretty as you are and she hasn't got a closetful of great clothes or all the latest records. But I feel comfortable around her, not as if I'm always trying to be what I think she wants me to be instead of what I am. I think you must know how I feel. I think you've felt it yourself, at least a little. You're terrific, Stacy," he said warmly, meeting her eyes. "But when I started thinking about it, I suppose I saw what everybody else saw all along: we don't have a single thing in common."

"Don't we?" she challenged him. "We seemed to have plenty in common all those nights we parked out by the lake."

"Sure, we've got *that* in common," he agreed. "We turn each other on like crazy. But is that a relationship? Stacy, we don't have anything to *talk* to each other about, not really. I know you did the best you could to work up an interest in cars and racing and my friends and all. You were willing to try harder than I was, and you should get some credit for that. But I could tell a lot of it was put on. I always knew you had to work at talking to me and saying the right things just as hard as I worked at talking to you. And it's stupid to keep on seeing each other with nothing in common except the physical stuff. I mean, where's that going to get us?"

"In trouble," she murmured, knowing Nick was right but wishing she could close her eyes and discover that this was all a nightmare. She squeezed her eyes tight, but when she opened them, the scene was still there, only blurred by her tears.

"I don't blame you for hating me," he said

softly, his hand on her shoulder. "And it's not like I don't want you, Stacy. I want you real bad—but in the wrong way. And I don't want to hurt you."

She nodded. "Look, Nick, I—I have to think about all this. I don't know how I feel right now." She smiled weakly. "But I know you're not some creep dropping me cold, and I suppose what you're saying might be right. Only . . . I don't want to talk about it any more right now, okay?"

"Okay." He stepped out of her way so she could unlock her car. "But, look, I'll give you a call on Sunday, all right?"

"Going out of town tomorrow?" she couldn't resist asking sweetly as she yanked the door open. She was helpless to stem the tide of jealousy washing over her. It was like nothing she had ever felt before. When Nick flushed and stared down at the parking lot, his smile replaced by a look of misery, she said simply, "Sunday's fine."

She got into the car, closed the door, and drove away, never looking back at Nick.

Unable to face the silent sterility of her room at home, Stacy drove through the side streets of Midvale and out into the flat stretches of the countryside where farmers' fields spread toward the horizon. She absently circled Brinton's Lake, barely noticing its stands of trees, leafless now that winter was fast approaching. The scenery might have been a painted backdrop against which she rushed past.

Shock kept her from crying. Horror nauseated her. More than once she slowed down and rolled her window partway open so the fresh cold air would keep her from becoming sick. How could this have happened to her?

At last, weak and shaking, she pulled her car to the side of the road, surprised to discover that she was at least fifteen minutes from Hawthorne Lane.

"Oh, Nick," she moaned aloud, the tears coming at last, "how could you do this to me? How?"

When her sobs quieted, she felt calmer and more controlled. But she still felt awful.

Nick's comments had made it clear Stacy was nothing but a novelty for him. And to think she'd risked so much—the cheerleading captainship, her friends, her popularity—for him!

She knew then what she'd have to do. Nick didn't know what a mistake he had made, but she didn't have time to explain it to him. She had a week before the election, before the assembly where the cheer squad performed their individual cheers. As long as everybody knew she and Nick were no longer an item, there would be no barrier in her path to retaining the captain's title. Much as she'd have preferred keeping her hurt to herself for a while, there was no question of it.

It was up to Stacy herself to make sure the

word got out about her and Nick Cooper. And the sooner the better.

With a sigh, she blew her nose and dried her eyes, then turned the key in the ignition and headed for home. She couldn't show up at Valerie's party the next night with eyes swollen from weeping.

FOURTEEN

It had been a long time since Stacy had gone out at night wearing anything but jeans and a sweater, and she had forgotten how much she liked dressing up. She wore her favorite party clothes: black jeans with a white silk shirt topped by a narrow black belt and the pearl necklace she had received for her sixteenth birthday. Black suede boots and a black cashmere sweater completed the outfit.

Valerie had the Masterses' guest house for entertaining, a converted coach house beyond the big Tudor. For a fleeting moment when Stacy arrived, she considered not ringing the doorbell, considered returning home to spend the evening in the silent peace of her own room. But the thought of the election caused her to press the doorbell instead. No sooner had Valerie opened the door to Stacy than her not-so-gentle teasing began.

"All alone?" Val asked, feigning surprise and peering over Stacy's shoulder into the night as if she expected someone to pop into view. "What happened? Nick find a car with a busted radiator that was just too fascinating to ignore?"

"No, it's not that," Stacy said, forcing a smile. Then an idea came to her, and the smile became a wide grin. Standing before her was the perfect opportunity to ensure that word spread quickly about her and Nick without her having to announce it to more than one person.

Moving closer to the other girl, Stacy lightly grasped her wrist. "If I tell you something, will you keep it between the two of us?" she asked softly.

"Of course, Stacy," Valerie vowed, her eyes sparkling coldly like matched aquamarines as she leaned closer.

In spite of her misery, Stacy almost burst out laughing. Valerie was always eager to be the first with gossip. Beneath her shiny hair, her ears must have perked up.

"Well, Nick and I have broken up," Stacy murmured. "As much as I wanted to avoid hurting him, I finally told him we were really wrong for each other."

"And here I was counting on your being able to get my car fixed for free!" Valerie complained, but she quickly patted Stacy's hand and said sweetly, "I didn't mean that, you know. I really am sorry, but it is good to see you here. We've missed you at all the parties lately. Come on, I'll get you a soda. And don't worry, I won't tell a soul!"

As Stacy followed her hostess across the spacious guest house with its high beamed ceiling, she marveled—not for the first time—at how Valerie could have so much and still feel the need to hurt other people. Didn't she realize how lucky she was?

Stacy took the ginger ale Valerie offered and retreated to a quiet spot on the sofa where she could watch for the next few minutes as Val scurried around whispering in one ear and then another, eager to spread Stacy's secret as quickly as possible. *The Masterses do know how to throw a party*, Stacy thought, surveying the strategically placed tubs of sodas and the numerous trays of crackers, raw vegetables, dips, and other munchies. And they spared no expense where Valerie was concerned. Stacy couldn't help wondering if they felt as threatened by their daughter's sharp tongue as her classmates did. Valerie probably wouldn't hesitate to make her own parents' lives miserable if she didn't get what she wanted.

As she sat alone, Stacy was almost self-conscious among the people she'd once thought of as her circle of friends. She wished Tess were there so she'd have somebody to cling to when she was feeling so fragile. But even though she'd given the go-ahead to friends like Tif and Joanie, Valerie was too stubborn, too conscious of her image, to invite Tess to a party of her own yet. She'd bide her time to make sure Tess realized how lucky she was when she finally did receive an invitation.

Stacy missed Gina, too, and she wondered why the other girl hadn't come, when she had hopes for the cheering election. It was a cheerleader's duty to attend gatherings like this, whether she wanted to or not. Gina was probably reluctant to come to Val's party if she had to leave early, and considering the Damones' restrictions, she probably would have. *Still, Gina's hurting herself with her standoffish behavior*, Stacy thought.

Across the room, Stacy spied Rich Stinson. Her pulse raced for a moment. He looked cuter than she remembered. Had it really been only two months since their breakup? The sight of his broad football-player's shoulders, sandy hair, and good-natured grin made Stacy wonder if she'd been hasty in giving him up so easily.

At his side she spotted Kathy Phillips, her hand gripped tightly in Rich's. One look at Kathy assured Stacy that the other girl was happier with Rich than she'd ever been.

Kathy was smiling up at Rich, her eyes wide with attention. The warm look he returned confirmed what Stacy had long suspected: she hadn't broken Rich's heart when she ended their relationship. Rich wasn't a guy who could survive without a girlfriend to confirm his own high opinion of himself. Stacy had been his first choice, but any popular and pretty girl would do.

I could have him back in a minute, she told herself. After all, wasn't it Rich who'd called Kathy Stacy's clone? But would Stacy really be happy with Rich now—or if she'd never given him up? She knew the answer was no. Maybe things with Nick hadn't ended as she had planned, but that didn't mean she'd be anything but bored if she were the girl whose hand Rich was holding tonight.

A heavy male hand on her shoulder startled her out of her daydreaming. "A little bird told me you're a free agent again," Dex Grantham crooned. He leaned toward her slightly, so she could smell the subtle, tangy scent of his aftershave and feel the soft caress of his cashmere crewneck as it brushed against her hand.

"A little vulture?" she asked coyly.

He laughed. "Don't let Valerie get to you, babe. She's not all that bad if you give her a chance. Life's not easy when you're used to getting what you want all the time, you know."

You don't have to tell me that, Stacy answered silently. Hadn't she taken Nick's loyalty to her for granted? Had it ever crossed her mind that he might be happier with somebody else?

Aloud, she just asked, "Like you?" and she was surprised when she heard the old flirtatious tone she'd always used with Dex creeping back into her voice. Maybe he was the most conceited individual she knew, but he was also the best-looking.

"Just like me," he agreed readily, smiling. "And right now, what I want is to dance with you."

He pulled her out into the center of the floor before she had time to protest, and she quickly set down the glass she'd been holding as they passed a table. Not that she would have put up much of a fight. She wanted to dance with Dex, and she wanted everyone to see her when she did it.

Only one thing was important right now. Not her feelings for Nick or her heartache at his dismissal of her. Not her disappointment that Rich had already found another cheerleader to replace her, either. Winning the cheering captain's election would take all her determination. And if that meant being a social butterfly, then she'd dance and laugh and smile and spread her wings until she was ready to collapse.

She danced with Dex and laughed with Val and greeted everybody who arrived, and she was shocked to look at her watch and discover it was midnight and time to leave.

She needed a good night's sleep to look her best for the next day's game. She had to turn in her best performance of the season at the last game before the election. But the friendly reception she'd received at Valerie's party had banished most of her worries. She counted on the captain's title remaining next to her name.

I can always think of a way to get Nick back after

I win, she told herself groggily as she drifted off to sleep. It wasn't as if he'd said he couldn't stand her. Let him have his little fling with Betty Ann. After that, she could make him realize that chemistry proved they were a perfect match.

When Nick called on Sunday, she was polite but distant. "I think we've both got some hard thinking to do," she said, sounding more controlled than she felt and glad he couldn't see how tightly she grasped the receiver to keep steady. "I think it's best if we don't see each other or talk for the next week or so. Maybe we'll both have our heads screwed on a little better then."

There, she thought with relief as she replaced the receiver. *Now I just have to give him time to start missing me.* And even if he didn't come back begging her to forgive him, this way their breakup had been a mutual decision instead of Nick's alone.

She went back to school on Monday resolving to renew all the friendships she had recently neglected. Friday's pep rally had shown her how much the other cheerleaders had begun ignoring her.

She resisted the impulse to deliver a lecture on proper squad behavior. It wasn't fair of them virtually to demote her just because they didn't approve of her boyfriend, but with the election so near, she couldn't afford to annoy anyone. She cheerfully endured practices, smiling widely even as she gritted her teeth and pretended not to notice how often the other girls excluded her from their huddles between cheers. Once the election was over, she could remind them what rank meant.

But there was no mistaking how Tess seemed to prefer the company of Gina and Patricia now, and Stacy was hurt. Captain or not, she had been Tess's best friend since kindergarten. Two months earlier, Stacy would have predicted that Tess would remain loyal even if every other Midvale student turned against her. Now that she was dating Dave Prentice, however, Tess had forgotten completely her old defense of techies and turned against Stacy just like every other Midvale snob. But Tess would soften soon. So would everyone else. They would have to when they saw how much of the old Harcourt sparkle Stacy still possessed.

When Thursday and the cheering election arrived, Stacy was not so sure of herself, especially when she noticed that even the juniors had created more original and difficult cheer routines than hers. As current captain, she cheered last. She sat through one routine after another, her nerves fraying as she listened to the crowd, praying she'd at least remember the words.

Gina, who cheered next to last, executed a complicated exercise that might have been an Olympic gymnastics routine. Stacy's heart sank as the gym filled with deafening applause when

Gina finished in a perfect split. It was Stacy's turn to perform.

Just remember, she reminded herself as she stood on shaky legs and prepared to run to the center of the gymnasium, *Gina's shy and quiet and you're outgoing and friendly.* It was popularity that won in the end, and while her fling with Nick had marred hers, it hadn't been irreparably damaged. Midvale wouldn't have paid such close attention to the romantic life of a less popular girl.

Her confidence grew as she sneaked glances at the stands during her routine. She had the undivided attention of a thousand Midvale students. As she began to jump, she poured all the energy of her worry and tension into her routine. She focused first on one section of bleachers, then the next, as if to say, "See, everybody, I'm still the same. I'm the Stacy Harcourt you made captain for this season. Isn't it clear I deserve it again?"

The clapping and cheering that broke loose when she ended her cheer convinced her she'd been forgiven for what her classmates saw as her mistake with Nick. It probably hadn't hurt her to have flirted with Dex Grantham a couple of times during the week. Stacy hadn't discouraged him when he hinted that he'd be happy to take Nick's place. As Dex winked at her from the bleachers, it didn't seem like such a bad idea. He was arrogant and rude, but he was also the hottest guy in all of Midvale.

Stacy daydreamed through the rest of the day. Students could vote any time before the end of the school day, and the winner would be announced at assembly Friday afternoon. By the end of the day, Stacy allowed her daydreams to wander to her plans for the basketball squad. Her schoolmates had seemed to make a real effort to catch up with her in the halls or to stop by her desk in class and tell her they had liked her cheer or that they thought she'd looked terrific. Maybe Nick's foolishness had happened at a good time. Stacy's unattached status could only help her win.

Of course, Gina Damone had easily outperformed Stacy. Even for someone as naturally athletic and graceful as Gina, that intricate routine must have taken hours of rigorous practice. Stacy couldn't have topped it even if she'd started practicing a cheer the first day of school—Gina was just too good. But Stacy hadn't won the cheering-captain election held the previous spring on cheering skills, either. Gina had bested her that time, too.

It was the same in any election: the best all-around won. No matter how talented Gina was, there were lots of people who thought she was cold and aloof. Before she'd known her, Stacy would have agreed. Now that she and Gina were fellow cheerleaders, Stacy saw past the other girl's mask of standoffishness and realized that Gina's reserve came from a combination of shyness and fear.

Still, the captain of any squad had to be the outgoing sort. Everyone knew that. It was doubly important when one of the cheerleaders was as reserved as Gina. And, as lovable and charming as Tess was, she just didn't have the polish required of a captain. The juniors, of course, never won the election for basketball or baseball season.

"And that leaves yours truly, Stacy Harcourt." She allowed herself to say it out loud, but not until she was in her car on the way home.

FIFTEEN

The next day there was a festive atmosphere in the halls of the school. The weekend's football game was to be played on Saturday afternoon, and by midmorning Friday, Stacy was thankful she wouldn't have to cheer that same night: the suspense was taking its toll on her. By the end of the pep rally that would close the assembly, she'd be ready for nothing more vigorous than a night in front of the TV set.

The attention of the other students, including more compliments on her cheer, helped soothe her anxiety and fire her anticipation.

Although it was no longer required, as it had been when some of Stacy's friends' parents were students at Midvale, it had become traditional for girls to wear dresses and boys to wear ties to assembly, and almost all the students observed the tradition. This assembly, of course, was the most important one of all, and Stacy's mother had come through brilliantly in the wardrobe department. Stacy wore a new pleated blue wool skirt, a matching high-necked blouse with tiny pleats down the front, and a deep blue knit sweater vest.

When she met the other squad members she was pleased to note that they had taken special pains to look their best, too. Gina was striking in a straight gray wool skirt and black Tyrolean jacket that showed off her elegant, small-boned figure; Tess, who'd once leaned toward puff-sleeved blouses and full skirts that had overemphasized her generous curves, now wore a simple burgundy corduroy tunic, thanks to Stacy's guidance. Her lavender eye shadow clashed a bit, but then, Tess wouldn't be Tess if she didn't stand out in some way.

The juniors, too, looked terrific: Sherri in a bold geometric print T-shirt dress that made her look attractively slender instead of just thin; Kathy in a skirt and blouse and vest combo, its similarity to her own no surprise to Stacy. Even Patricia, who had been a wiry little tomboy back when she was known as Pixie, looked feminine and grown-up in a lace-collared sweater and corduroy skirt. On this day, being a cheerleader was something to be extra proud of, something to flaunt.

As she was coming out of chemistry class, Stacy saw Nick standing by a row of lockers about fifty feet down the corridor, talking to a couple of his auto-body buddies. Her heart in her throat, Stacy saw him as if for the first time: how irresistible he looked in dark cords with a blue oxford shirt and a skinny black leather tie. Turning sharply, she walked out of her way to avoid meeting him. She couldn't worry about Nick until later, after the election results were announced.

At lunchtime, Stacy found Gina, Janet, and three other seniors seated at the usual table. She joined them, but she couldn't concentrate on the conversation. She supposed Gina, too, was feeling the tension as the day wore on, though it was hard to tell, since Gina was normally quiet anyway. Stacy picked at her lunch and wished for a way to speed the passage of the afternoon while Janet discussed the *Sentinel's* problems in covering the assembly.

It wasn't until she was almost ready to leave that Tess's absence from their usual table struck Stacy. She'd grown so used to Tess skipping lunch to practice cheers that she hadn't remembered there was no longer any need to practice during lunch hour.

Then she saw her. Tess was sharing a small table in the corner with Patricia. Couldn't Tess see that Stacy was back and be her best friend once again? Tess's petty snub could spoil her own carefully constructed popularity if people saw her so thick with a junior.

After an excruciating fifth period, Stacy had to stop herself from running to the auditorium. But she'd ended up walking with Valerie and Tif, so she saw no polite way to get out of sitting with them. It wasn't until Valerie talked someone out of saving three seats that Stacy recalled how she and Tess had once saved seats for each other. Stacy saw Tess's familiar curly head several rows to the front, between Janet's buzz cut and Patricia's unmistakable carroty shag.

The teachers' speeches were, as usual, a yawn and a half. As the starting players for Saturday's football game were called to the stage one by one, Stacy's interest sharpened. She smiled when she saw Dave wink in Tess's direction as he loped up the aisle, but that smile faded when Rich stood at the mention of his name and she recognized Kathy Phillips in the seat next to him.

At last the moment arrived when Ms. Bowen stood at the lectern. But even she prolonged Stacy's anxiety, congratulating the football team on its efforts.

"Before I announce the results of the winter season's cheering-captain election," she finally said, "I'd like all the cheerleaders to come up on stage as I call their names. This is your chance to show your appreciation to these six girls, who have helped rouse the Mustangs to victory with their dedication and enthusiasm.

"All six of these girls deserve a special title," she went on with feeling. "Cheering is more than getting out there on the field and screaming your lungs out. A cheerleader is the embodiment of good school spirit, of the desire to excel. Cheerleaders have a tremendous responsibility. It's up to these girls to make sure each and every one of you supports our teams. They practice long and hard, give up a great deal to be on the squad, and represent the best qualities in our student body: leadership, dedication, and faith in Midvale High School. Please give them each a well-deserved round of applause as I call their names."

One by one, the cheerleaders made their way to the stage, each responding in her own way to the clapping and cheering that greeted her name: Gina's expression was blank with what Stacy suspected was a case of stage fright; Tess flushed with pleasure; Patricia, still pixielike in spite of her name change, skipped to the stage waving at her friends; Sherri wafted forward effortlessly; and Kathy strode to the front of the auditorium with confidence.

Stacy concentrated on smiling gratefully and looking calm as she climbed up on stage, behavior she thought fitting for the squad's captain.

"And now it give me great pleasure to announce that the student body has again seen fit to elect Stacy Harcourt as captain of the cheering squad for basketball season!"

Stacy's mind went blank with relief. She'd won! She'd really won. She should have known her position was in no real jeopardy. Grinning triumphantly, Stacy took a few shaky steps forward toward Ms. Bowen and the microphone. The new captain always said a few words of thanks to the student body.

She stopped dead in her tracks, her smile faltering, as she realized Ms. Bowen had more to say.

"And it gives me equal pleasure," the cheering coach went on, "to say that this season, for the first time in the history of our school, you've seen fit to elect cocaptains. The other captain elected in this tie is Gina Damone!"

Stunned, Stacy felt Gina break out of line behind her and start for the front of the stage. Somehow Stacy managed to put one foot in front of the other, to continue her short journey to the lectern.

It couldn't be! How could they expect her, after having had the captaincy all to herself for months, to suddenly share it with another cheerleader? It was unheard of!

Of course it wasn't Gina's fault she'd won, Stacy realized, observing Gina's tear-filled eyes and overflowing happiness. But it wasn't Stacy's, either. It was those people who sat in the bleachers, her supposed friends, who'd seen fit to punish her for mixing with the wrong crowd.

In what Stacy hoped looked like good manners, she motioned to Gina to make her acceptance speech. Stacy needed time to regain her self-control. The last thing she could afford was to offend anyone by sounding like a poor sport and showing her resentment.

"Thank you, thank you, thank you!" Gina said with a rush of feeling Stacy couldn't recall ever having heard in her voice before. "I can't believe this! It's a great honor, and I promise I'll do the best I can to make everyone proud of me as cocaptain. And, of course," she added, her slight Italian accent creeping through in her excitement, "it's wonderful to be sharing this captain's spot with Stacy Harcourt. I know I can learn a lot from her."

A few titters reached Stacy's ears after the last sentence, and she knew all too well what was amusing some of the crowd: they were poking one another in the ribs and saying, sure, Stacy Harcourt could teach Gina a thing or two, and not just about cheerleading.

As coolly as possible, she took her place behind the microphone, concentrating hard on sounding gracious, on concealing her disappointment. She uttered some brief words of thanks for the support of her fellow students, then said, "I look forward to being next season's cocaptain with Gina. In my eyes, there's never been a single captain of this squad. We all share the work and the joys and the rewards and the credit. Thank you all!"

Then, so everybody could see just what a terrific sport she was, she leaned over and kissed Gina loudly on the cheek.

When the formal part of the assembly ended, Stacy was the first one off the stage, hurrying down the corridor that led to the locker room. She had no time to stand around letting everyone congratulate her—or, more accurately, let them rub it in. Her election had, in fact, been a demotion, from full captain to one of two. But no one would ever see that she wasn't thrilled, no matter how much they might suspect the truth.

By the time the rest of the squad arrived to change, Stacy was already on her way to the gym in her uniform. She ran through the cheer schedule with Ms. Bowen, not trusting herself alone with the rest of the squad. Especially Tess. No doubt Tess Belding was feeling pretty smug just then. After all, hadn't Tess predicted Stacy would be unseated?

Stacy's cheering at this rally was as good as it had ever been. She hurled herself whole-heartedly into each separate routine. Her single-minded concentration wasn't the result of any desire to excel this time: she was just doing her best to blot out her shame and fury.

At least you're still a captain, she told herself in the brief pauses between cheers. Since she and Gina had tied, then Gina could have had the captaincy all to herself with just one more vote.

So the kids had found a way to show her they hadn't forgotten her fling with Nick Cooper. This was one revenge plot that would backfire. Stacy was more determined than ever to win Nick back. When she and Nick became a steady item again, she'd show those snobs who controlled Stacy Harcourt's life.

By the time the pep rally came to a close, Stacy had made a reluctant peace with the situation. She truly liked Gina. She'd be foolish not to accept her technical advice. And she was grateful she hadn't been entirely defeated. But when she and Nick were together again, she would flaunt her relationship with him in front of all the people who'd voted against her.

When the rally ended she was ready to face the rest of the squad. But this time, Ms. Bowen wanted to talk to her, to discuss a change in cheers for the game the next day. By the time Stacy hurried to the locker room to change, it appeared deserted.

Only after she'd changed back into her skirt did she hear a soft sobbing coming from behind a row of lockers. It was a familiar sound, one that had brought sympathetic tears from Stacy herself many times in the past dozen years.

She walked down the row and peered around the corner. There was Tess, collapsed atop one of the benches in a heap that threatened to leave her dress in a wrinkled mess. Stacy almost turned and sneaked away. Then she stopped herself.

Rushing over, she sank down next to Tess and patted her gently on the shoulder. "Come on, Tess," she said softly, "don't cry. Maybe you'll win the election for baseball season. After all, the whole school must realize how hard you work and how much you try. Don't let it get you down. They can't have a three-way captaincy among all the seniors on the squad, can they?"

"What are you talking about?" Tess sat up abruptly and took her hands away from her face. Within rings of smeared eye makeup her eyes were wide with puzzlement. "You think I expected to be captain?"

"Well, you're crying, aren't you?" Stacy asked, confused.

Tess laughed sharply through her tears. "Do you think for one minute I'd expect to be elected captain of the whole squad? For Pete's sake, Stacy, I'm thrilled just being a cheerleader! I don't want to be the captain."

"I don't understand. If you didn't care about winning the election, then why are you crying?"

"Because my stupid parents are getting a divorce!" A fresh burst of tears punctuated her words. "Do you think the only things that are important are the things that matter to *you*?"

"Of course not, Tess," Stacy murmured. "Of course I don't. Oh, Tess, I'm so sorry! I should have known something serious was wrong!" Stacy's voice was troubled and sincere. "You're right to think I've been an awful friend. I guess I just got so caught up in Nick I forgot my old friends were just as important. But I promise it'll never happen again. I'll never let Nick become the center of my existence."

Tess stared up, jolted out of her own misery. "Nick? But I thought you'd broken up!"

Stacy shrugged. "Well, we did. But I'm sure

I can get him back." She laughed bitterly. "Although I guess I should be mad at him for not giving me the brushoff earlier, when I might still have won the election on my own. Still, I can't wait to show those kids who voted against me!"

"You mean you really believe you didn't get the captaincy all to yourself because the kids were mad at you for going with a techie? Get serious, Stacy! Nobody at Midvale ever took you and Nick seriously. Everybody knew sooner or later you'd get bored with dating a guy you had nothing in common with. If the two of you do get back together again, no one's going to expect it to last."

"Well, then, how come I didn't win the election?"

"That had nothing to do with Nick, Stacy." Tess was shaking her head in astonishment. "Can't you see the truth yet? Gina worked *hard* to win, Stacy; she showed that cheerleading and being chosen captain really mattered to her."

"And what did I do?" Stacy asked stiffly.

"You did a simple cheer, one of the easiest routines I've ever seen. Sure, you did it all right, but Gina showed she cared enough to work up a *great* routine in spite of the fact that she's easily the best cheerleader on the squad. To tell the truth, I expected Gina to win completely. I guess being the prettiest and most popular girl in school still counts for something."

"You're just trying to make me feel bad for letting you down," Stacy protested weakly.

"Don't you know me better than that, Stacy? It's not Nick everybody was against—it's the way you acted after you met him. You dropped everyone."

"Well, what was I supposed to do? Drag Nick to parties and the pizza parlor with me?"

"Sure. Why not?"

"Because it's not Nick's type of thing. He has nothing in common with that crowd, Tess. He'd have been bored stiff. Besides, everyone would have given him the cold shoulder."

"That's not true. People here give everyone a chance, whether they're college prep or techies. You're the one who's busy labeling people, Stacy. Are you sure you weren't afraid Nick's being bored with your kind of fun wouldn't make him wonder if he was bored with you, too? And weren't you bored enough with his interests that you expected your other friends to feel the same way?"

"No, Tess! That's absolutely not true!"

"I think you liked being seen with Nick," Tess said simply. "I think you liked his looks and thought he was sexy and were intrigued by his coming from another world. But, remember, I knew him first, so I know what he's like. And as nice a guy as Nick is, you'll never convince me you're crazy about black leather jackets and heavy-metal bands and the speedway. You must have been bored out of your mind by him!"

"That's not true . . ." Stacy began, but the

moment she heard the weakness in her own protest, she stopped short.

"And now you're talking about trying to get him back?" Tess shook her head and laughed, mopping at her eyes, which were almost dry now, and trying to wipe off the half-moons of purple makeup beneath them. "Boy, I thought my folks were crazy, but you win hands down!"

"I truly *am* sorry about your mother and father," Stacy told her friend, squeezing her hand. "I guess I've been a lousy friend lately, haven't I? At least you and Dave seem happy."

"I don't know what I'd do without him!" Tess assured her fervently. "He's been an angel. But are you serious about trying to get Nick back?"

Stacy smiled slightly. "I guess not. The more I think about it, the more I doubt if he'd want me back. Nick kind of knew all along that we were wrong for each other. About the only thing we both liked to do was park. I still think he's incredibly attractive. But I guess that's one reason for staying away from him. It was just a matter of time before we would have gone too far."

"You mean you really almost did it?"

"Oh, Tess." Stacy felt a rush of the old confidence she and Tess used to share. "We didn't actually plan on doing anything. But we were getting closer and closer to the point where I don't know if I could have said no." Stacy sighed. "Our chemistry was so perfect I guess it didn't matter to me that we had so little to talk about. But now I know I'd have always been sorry if I'd gone too far with a boy just because of physical attraction. It's not enough. Nick's probably a lot happier with this girl he's going out with now from Brownville. I guess I just wanted him back for my own reasons."

"Some things just aren't meant to be," Tess said softly. "At least that's what Mom keeps telling me about her and Dad." She took a deep breath, as if she was afraid she'd start crying all over again. "But don't worry, Stacy, you'll find someone else."

"I know," Stacy agreed. "But I don't think I want to rush into another relationship right away. I think I'd better get to know myself a lot better before I start getting close to any boy. It's sort of embarrassing to realize my friends know me better in some ways than I know myself."

"You won't be bored without a boyfriend?"

Stacy shook her head. "I didn't have any excuse for being bored in the first place. I was head of the cheering squad, I had great friends, I really had everything. What right did I have to be bored?" She paused. "You know, the night of Valerie's party I was asking myself how Valerie could be such a troublemaker when she's got everything in the world. Now I can see how easy it is."

"I'm not sure having everything you ever needed is a great excuse for being mean. But I've never heard you sound so together before.

Dating Nick sure made you think a lot of things through."

"Oh, this, too, shall pass," Stacy joked. "I wasn't all that aware of how I felt when I was with Nick. I was still too wrapped up in the fabulous Stacy Harcourt then. You know, right before I met Nick, I was feeling real sorry for myself, at the way my life was all mapped out for me. Maybe I just *thought* it was that way. Dating Nick has made me see that I've got a lot of different choices I can make. I was so busy feeling trapped I didn't see the only thing trapping me was myself."

"Oh, Stace, I'm glad we're friends again," Tess said. "And I'm glad you're still the same old Stacy, even if you've changed in some ways."

"Me, too," Stacy said as the two girls embraced.

"Come on." Tess stood up. "We'd better get back to homeroom and check in if we want to get out of here."

"Want to stop for a soda on the way home?" Stacy asked.

"I'd like that," Tess said. "And, Stacy, I don't want you to think I blamed our falling out all on you. It was my fault, too. I was so caught up in what was going on at home I never thought that you might need a friend, too. You seemed so controlled in everything."

"Well, I did think you were kind of hard on me," Stacy said. "But I'm glad I've finally realized that no matter what happens, I'll always need my friends. No one is worth giving up friends for."

"Speaking of friends," Tess began, "maybe when we get to Nicola's we should put our heads together and try to figure out a way to help Gina. I swear that girl's going to go off the deep end if she doesn't get asked for a date soon."

"She doesn't know how much trouble she's in for when she gets one!" Stacy said. "But I guess we've all got to learn for ourselves."

As the two friends walked arm in arm through the locker room and into the hall, the image of the butterfly caught in glass came suddenly to Stacy's mind. She knew now that the freedom she'd once hoped for was just beginning.

SWEET DREAMS are fresh, fun and exciting,—alive with the flavor of the contemporary teen scene—the joy and doubt of *first love*. If you've missed any SWEET DREAMS titles, from #1 to #100, then you're missing out on *your* kind of stories, written about people like *you*!

☐ 24837	DAY DREAMER #32	$2.25
	Janet Quin-Harkin	
☐ 24336	FORBIDDEN LOVE #35	$2.25
	Marian Woodruff	
☐ 24338	SUMMER DREAMS #36	$2.25
	Barbara Conklin	
☐ 24340	FIRST LOVE #39	$2.25
	Debra Spector	
☐ 24838	THE TRUTH ABOUT ME AND BOBBY V. #41	$2.25
	Janetta Johns	
☐ 24341	DREAM PROM #45	$2.25
	Margaret Burman	
☐ 24688	SECRET ADMIRER #81	$2.25
	Debra Spector	
☐ 24383	HEY, GOOD LOOKING #82	$2.25
	Jane Polcovar	
☐ 24823	LOVE BY THE BOOK #83	$2.25
	Anne Park	
☐ 24718	THE LAST WORD #84	$2.25
	Susan Blake	
☐ 24890	THE BOY SHE LEFT BEHIND #85	$2.25
	Suzanne Rand	
☐ 24945	QUESTIONS OF LOVE #86	$2.25
	Rosemary Vernon	
☐ 24824	PROGRAMMED FOR LOVE #87	$2.25
	Marion Crane	
☐ 24891	WRONG KIND OF BOY #88	$2.25
	Shannon Blair	
☐ 24946	101 WAYS TO MEET MR. RIGHT #89	$2.25
	Janet Quin-Harkin	
☐ 24992	TWO'S A CROWD #90	$2.25
	Diana Gregory	
☐ 25070	THE LOVE HUNT #91	$2.25
	Yvonne Green	
☐ 25131	KISS & TELL #92	$2.25
	Janet Quin-Harkin	
☐ 25071	THE GREAT BOY CHASE #93	$2.25
	Janet Quin-Harkin	
☐ 25132	SECOND CHANCES #94	$2.25
	Nancy Levinso	
☐ 25178	NO STRINGS ATTACHED #95	$2.25
	Eileen Hehl	
☐ 25179	FIRST, LAST, AND ALWAYS #96	$2.25
	Barbara Conklin	

Prices and availability subject to change without notice.

A LOVE TRILOGY

First there is <u>LOVING</u>.

Meet Caitlin, gorgeous, rich charming and wild. And anything Caitlin wants she's used to getting. So when she decides that she wants handsome Jed Michaels, there's bound to be some trouble. ☐ 24716/$2.95

Then there is <u>LOVE LOST</u>.

The end of term has arrived and it looks like the summer will be a paradise. But tragedy strikes and Caitlin's world turns upside down. Will Caitlin speak up and risk sacrificing the most important thing in her life?
☐ 25130/$2.95

And at last, <u>TRUE LOVE</u>.

Things are just not going the way Caitlin had planned, and she can't seem to change them! Will it take a disaster and a near-fatality for people to see the light?
☐ 25295/$2.95

Prices and availability subject to change without notice.

Buy them at your local bookstore or use this handy coupon for ordering:

Shop at home
for quality childrens books
and save money, too.

Now you can order books for the whole family from Bantam's latest listing of hundreds of titles including many fine children's books. *And* this special offer gives you an opportunity to purchase a Bantam book for only 50¢. Here's how:

By ordering any five books at the regular price per order, you can also choose any other single book listed (up to $4.95 value) for just 50¢. Some restrictions do apply, so for further details send for Bantam's listing of titles today.

☐	25143	**POWER PLAY #4**	$2.50
☐	25043	**ALL NIGHT LONG #5**	$2.50
☐	25105	**DANGEROUS LOVE #6**	$2.50
☐	25106	**DEAR SISTER #7**	$2.50
☐	25092	**HEARTBREAKER #8**	$2.50
☐	25026	**RACING HEARTS #9**	$2.50
☐	25016	**WRONG KIND OF GIRL #10**	$2.50
☐	25046	**TOO GOOD TO BE TRUE #11**	$2.50
☐	25035	**WHEN LOVE DIES #12**	$2.50
☐	24524	**KIDNAPPED #13**	$2.25
☐	24531	**DECEPTIONS #14**	$2.50
☐	24582	**PROMISES #15**	$2.50
☐	24672	**RAGS TO RICHES #16**	$2.50
☐	24723	**LOVE LETTERS #17**	$2.50
☐	24825	**HEAD OVER HEELS #18**	$2.50
☐	24893	**SHOWDOWN #19**	$2.50
☐	24947	**CRASH LANDING! #20**	$2.50

Prices and availability subject to change without notice.

Buy them at your local bookstore or use this handy coupon for ordering:

Bantam Books, Inc., Dept SVH, 414 East Golf Road, Des Plaines, Ill. C0016

Please send me the books I have checked above. I am enclosing $_____
(please add $1.25 to cover postage and handling). Send check or money order
—no cash or C.O.D.'s please.

Mr/Mrs/Miss _____

Address_____

City_____ State/Zip_____

SVH—11/85

Please allow four to six weeks for delivery. This offer expires 5/86.